Chords of Love

More by Janetta Fudge Messmer

Early Birds
Southbound Birds

Chords of Love

Janetta Fudge Messmer

Chords of Love

Front cover design by Janice Thompson.
Remaining cover design by Crystal L Barnes.

Dedication

To Janice: Start to finish, you saw me through it. To Doris: Best friend, neighbor, and person who kept on me to finish the project. Thank you both.

My Lord and Savior. Thank you for answering my prayers. Writing without You is unthinkable.

One

Central City, Colorado
August 10, 1890

"Mark my word, Abigail. It's going to take a miracle for your mama to love Colorado now."

Abby could only venture a guess that her parents had discussed the opera house. Again. The very one which sat in ruins on the main street in Central City. And the only reason Mama agreed to come west.

Shifting in her side saddle, Abby yanked on Herkimer's reins and offered a firm, "Whoa, boy," to bring him to a halt. She glanced at her father and thought it best to bridle her tongue about her mother's antics the day before. More than once her hasty words got her in trouble.

"Daughter, is there something you want to tell me?" Papa slowed his horse to a stop next to her.

Abigail had to tell him the latest or she'd burst at the seams. Without a moment's hesitation she said, "Papa, we've only lived here a little more than a month, but what I heard

Mama say to the owner of Presley Mercantile yesterday is sure to twist the ends of your moustache."

Papa turned in his saddle. "What did she say this time?"

Abigail cleared her throat and sat higher in her side-saddle. "Now, remember, Papa, I'm quoting Mama. She said, 'Mr. Noah Presley, I despise this dirty, desolate town of yours.'"

Her father's eyes twinkled as he glanced sideways at her. Abby knew she'd gotten away with a little sassiness on their riding excursion, but when they returned to Central City, one of his stern looks would shush her right up.

"Oh, how I love that woman." Papa chuckled, then his expression grew more stern. "But tell me she really didn't say those things." He stroked Dancer's neck. His horse stayed steady on the rocky path leading out of the little mining town.

"Yes, and there's more, Papa. You'd better hold tight to the reins for this one." Abigail did the same, as if she needed to get ready, too. "Mama also told Mr. Presley, 'You people can't even keep your opera house running. It's simply disgraceful.'"

"Oh, heaven's mercy. . ." Her father's voice trailed off.

Abigail let him absorb the news for a bit, while she lifted her eyes to the wondrous view stretched out before her. The snowcapped peaks of the Rocky Mountains and their exquisite beauty filled her with awe and wonder.

"Daughter, did you hear a single word I said?"

"Oh yes, Papa. Heard every word." She smiled as she gave her father a loving pat on his arm.

"Well then, dear, what do you suggest we do to help make your mama happy? I'm afraid until the opera house is up and running again, nothing will change her mind."

"I don't know, but my guess is, if Mama's not happy,

none of us will be either." Abigail giggled, but her father's expression held none of his earlier merriment.

To escape possible reprisal, Abigail slapped Herkimer's hind-quarter. The move spooked him and he reared up. If she hadn't held on, she would have catapulted off his back. She and her riding outfit would have landed in one of the mud puddles, along with her pride.

Abigail's father snickered, but she ignored him as she straightened her fitted jacket. Once again secure, she turned Herkimer toward Central City. This time at a slower pace. Her papa followed, still chuckling.

Go ahead and laugh, Papa, you aren't the one she expects to sing in front of everyone—if and when the opera house is refurbished.

A shiver ran down Abigail's spine and continued clear down to her toes when the subject of her singing came into the conversation. She agreed to practice, but getting on the stage? Never. Falling flat on her face years ago had cured Abby from ever attempting a performance again.

Her parent's encouragement didn't alleviate her fears either. She'd told them, "I love you both with all my heart, and don't mean any disrespect, but God Himself will have to carry me on the stage if He wants me to sing on it."

"Daughter, the scowl you're wearing on your pretty face is going to make your mama think we're mad at each other."

Papa's voice broke into Abigail's thoughts and she said, "We wouldn't want that." She winked at her father. "Oh, ouch."

"What is it?" He reached for Abigail's reins.

"I'm okay, Papa. Some sweat got in my eyes." She took off her hat and fanned herself. "Oh, how I do wish women didn't have to wear all these layers when they went out riding."

Her papa licked his fingers and twirled the ends of his moustache, which Abigail knew as his sign that he didn't want to discuss the subject of trousers. Especially when a woman brought it up.

"We need to get on home. I think I hear your mama calling your name." Papa prodded Dancer and took off in the direction of town.

Abigail stuffed her hat back on her head and in a huff followed him, muttering for all to hear. "All I'm getting at is it's hot in this ridiculous getup. If I could wear a pair of your pants, I'm sure they'd be cooler and more comfortable than this."

"Daughter, you might as well quit blabbering. I can't hear a word you're saying."

Abigail knew her papa heard every word she'd spoken, but instead of being accused of more feistiness, she dropped the subject. She'd broach the clothing issue on another outing.

Or maybe not. Maybe she could find an old, worn out pair of his trousers that Mama would have stuffed in the rag bag. Abigail could give them a try. In the confines of her bedroom, of course.

Satisfied with her plan, Abigail enjoyed the scenery in front of her once again. The mountain ranges provided her a little taste of heaven each time she gazed upon them. Her heart overflowed with thanksgiving.

She began to fidget in her side-saddle as a hymn bubbled up inside her. But, she'd have to refrain from belting it out today. They were too close to town and someone might hear her singing to her Savior.

As she and Papa turned on Eureka Street, she caught sight of Mama standing on their front stoop and she said, "Papa, she doesn't lo—"

"Miss Abigail Jane Thompson," Her mother's voice carried over the sound of the horses' hooves on the cobble stone street. As they drew closer, she continued. "Otto Thompson, you should be ashamed of yourself. Your daughter's late for her music lesson, again."

"Sorry, dear. Time got away from me." Papa glanced at Abigail and smiled. "Ivy, I've got an idea. Next time we go riding, you come with us. We'll show you some awful pretty country you would never see in Dallas."

"Mama, he's right. The Rockies. They're absolutely breathtaking."

"I'm sure they are, but I've lived thirty-nine years without these mountains and I'm sure I'll live a few more if I choose not to go into them. Anyway, I can see them perfectly from the porch." Mama turned and strode up the three stairs of their Victorian home. When she reached the front door, she twirled around, pointed with her right hand and said, "See."

"You don't know what you're missing." Papa got off Dancer and headed for the stable. Abigail jumped off and let go of Herkimer and the mare followed.

Abby sauntered to the porch and took off her hat. With a little too much theatrics, she leaned over and smoothed down the wrinkles on her riding skirt. She knew the more time she dilly-dallied, the later her music lesson would start.

She finally finished her primping and sneaked a peek at her mother. Her frown told Abigail that she and Papa would catch a mountain of trouble later, but her music lesson came first. Nothing, other than breathing, rated more important in her mama's life.

Two

Once they made it inside the house, and Abigail changed out of her riding outfit, the dreaded music lesson began. Mama's lovely soprano voice filled the parlor as she began to sing. Abby joined in and their two voices melded together as one.

That was until Mama rapped her baton on the piano and said, "No, no, no, daughter, try again. You only have a month to perfect this before Homecoming Sunday."

The urge to run out of the parlor screaming almost overtook Abigail. And if she heard the word "Homecoming Sunday" one more time, she didn't know if she could keep her feet inside their Victorian home.

Abby would rather go fetch her friend, Mollie Blair. Have Mama teach her how to sing. Might be a challenge, though. The young woman thought she sounded as sweet as a song bird when she sang. Truth be told, she couldn't carry a tune in a bucket to save her soul.

With her mind made up, Abigail decided to talk to her

mother. She paused to choose the words carefully then began. "Mama. . ."

The sound of the door knocker saved her from saying something that could get her into a heap of stew.

Her father's loving voice rang out. "Well, Mr. Presley, do come in. What a pleasant surprise." Papa ushered the storekeeper into the parlor. The hot June breeze followed the handsome man inside.

Abigail picked up a piece of sheet music and fanned herself. Her nose tickled when she caught a whiff of cinnamon and sugar. She eyed Noah Presley, the owner of the local mercantile, but the delicious-looking pastry balanced on his right hand lured her attention away from him and his gorgeous blue-gray eyes.

"What do you have there? Smells wonderful." Abigail piped up from across the spacious room.

"Abigail Jane," Her mother's tone quieted further inquiries.

"Mrs. Thompson, this here apple pie is for you. I heard it's your favorite." Noah smiled in Mama's direction, and then shifted his gaze to Abby. His cheeks reddened a little when their eyes met. Her tummy did a little jitter, too.

Oh, what is wrong with me? He's much too old. He told me he'd be twenty-four years old Christmas Day.

Abby did her best to keep her gaze on the pie.

"Thank you, Mr. Presley. I do have a weakness for apple," Mama said with a smile. She turned to Abigail. "Daughter, do you really think my personal likes and dislikes need to be discussed down at the mercantile? I don't, thank you very much."

Abby cleared her throat and felt her cheeks warm.

Mama turned to face Noah. "Anyway, Mr. Presley, have a

nice day." Mama grabbed the pie, dishtowel and all, and headed toward the kitchen. The sound of her heeled boots echoed across the dining room floor.

"Noah, please forgive my wife. She's been a little out of sorts since our move here. Under normal circumstances, she wouldn't be so terse with our guests."

"Especially one who brought her an apple pie," Abigail added and then chuckled. She turned to her father. "Papa, it doesn't look like anything's going to change Mama's attitude."

"Shush, daughter."

"Sorry."

Abigail tidied up the music on the top of the grand piano while the store owner and her papa spoke. Once when she glanced over at Mr. Presley, Abby caught him looking her way. Getting caught must have caused him to blush, because he almost glowed.

Noah quickly turned his attention back to her father, but not before Abigail caught sight of the cute dimple on his right cheek. *Yes, he does have such a sweet smile.*

"Sir, I must be on my way. Work awaits."

"Thank you again for the pie, Noah, and please forgive my wife's curtness."

"It's not a problem. No offense taken. I hope your family enjoys the dessert." Noah moved toward the front door. He stopped and shifted his weight from one foot to the other. "Sir, I wanted to welcome all of you to Central City."

"Thank you, son. We appreciate the warm welcome. Don't we, Abigail?" Papa smiled.

Lots of things went through her mind before she answered. And what came out took the wind right out of the conversation. Abigail cleared her throat and asked, "Is your father planning to fix the opera house? If he does, when will it open?"

Lord, please have him tell us he's not fixing it.

The color left Noah's cheeks and he nodded. She didn't know if he agreed with her or just acknowledged her statement, but she could tell he didn't seem pleased with her line of questioning.

"Miss Thompson, I'm not sure what's going on. But I know one thing, it sounded like a night at the opera house when I came up to your door. Is that one of the beautiful songs you were singing?" His hand shook as he pointed to the sheets of music Abby held in her hand.

"Heavens no, Mr. Presley." Abigail's mama appeared at the doorway. "It's obvious your ears aren't trained to know the difference between musical scales and an aria. I'm curious, does your father know anything about running an opera house?"

Noah spun around and headed to the front door. He opened it and looked as if he'd leave without answering the question. Still at the door he said, "Who knows what my pop is up to? Don't ask me. Hope to see you in church tomorrow." He left, closing the door hard behind him.

Abigail glanced at her parents. Her mother's mouth stood wide open, obviously posed to say something, but nothing came out. Mama waltzed over to the piano and picked up a piece of music and fanned herself. Papa turned to leave the parlor.

Before he got too far Mama said, "See, Otto, these people here in this God-forsaken country do not have a stitch of manners." She laid the music down and walked to the front door. As she opened it the edge of the curtain fell back into its intended place.

"Dear, I don't think Noah's manners have a bit to do with

his quick exit. Something's going on with him and his papa."

"Now, Otto, promise me you aren't going to go snooping around. Anyway, let's not worry about the Presley's right now. Supper's ready. I heated up some soup for us, a lighter fare since we have a special dessert tonight." A hint of a smile turned up the edges of her lips.

"I'm happy to see Mr. Presley's gift lightened your mood." Contentment registered in Papa's eyes. "But, dear, I do believe you nearly scared a few years off the young man when you grabbed the pie out of his hand."

"I don't know what came over me." Mama blushed. "I hope you apologized for *my* bad manners."

"Yes, I did, but enough of that. Where is the infamous pie? Or, have you already gobbled it up and left Abigail and me to lick the plate?" Papa took steps in her direction and put his arms around her waist. "And about me snooping, I'm just curious. That's all."

"Uh-huh." Mama gave him a kiss on his cheek and headed to the kitchen. He followed close behind. Abigail heard her father assuring her mother he'd not get involved with these *uncivilized* people here in Colorado.

Abby grinned as she listened to her parents' tomfoolery. She knew if she hadn't been in the room, her papa would have given her mother an affectionate pat on her backside, something she'd seen him do more than once when he didn't think anyone else was watching.

Lord, I'm not looking for a husband, but if You have one picked out for me I'd like him to be just like Papa.

"Daughter, are you coming to supper tonight?"

Her father's question interrupted her daydreaming about her future beau. "Yes, Papa, I'm on my way. When I get there I better not find any of Mr. Presley's apple pie missing. I know how you are."

Hearty laughter greeted her ears as she joined her parents in the kitchen. When she caught sight of her father leaning over her dish of tempting dessert, his fork poised to take a bite, her giggles matched his.

"Don't you dare." Abby waggled her finger in Papa's direction.

"Otto, would you please leave our daughter's food alone? I do declare. What gets into you sometimes?" Mama picked up the ladle and scooped out three helpings of chicken noodle soup.

"Here Mama, let me help you." Abigail walked over to the counter and picked up the bowls. As she placed her father's in front of him, she kissed him on the forehead and whispered, "You're ornery."

"Just like someone else I know."

Abigail chuckled as she slid in next to her mother on the bench seat. Papa took her and Mama's hands and blessed their meal. She hoped he'd hurry. The savory aroma of Mama's cooking mingled with the sweet smell of Mr. Presley's dessert made Abigail's stomach rumble. She couldn't wait to dig in and forget music lessons and the opera house for a little while.

Three

"Yes, Mrs. Thompson, I'm well aware of the difference between a musical scale and an aria," Noah Presley muttered the words while he stocked the bottom shelf of the mercantile. He couldn't believe the woman's audacity a few days earlier, accusing him of such.

"Ma'am, thanks to Grandma P., music has graced my ears since the day the good Lord put me on this earth." The store owner pushed the can of beans with more force than intended and the lot of them toppled over. "She doesn't have a clue what she's talkin'—"

"Mr. Presley, excuse me."

Noah's jabbering came to a halt when he heard the female voice. Seconds later, something tapped him on the bottom of his boot. When he lay on his stomach to fill the lower shelves, he didn't realize his size 12 feet stuck out from under the curtain between the back room and the front of the mercantile. He scrambled to stand up and flung open the divider and said, "May I help y—"

Miss Abigail Thompson stood smack dab in front of him,

her nose a mere two inches from his chest. The only thing Noah could see of the new arrival was the top of her flowered bonnet and some blond curls peeking out from underneath the wide brim.

He stepped back after he recovered from almost knocking the attractive girl flat on her behind. Abigail did the same, then tilted her head to look up at him.

"Yes, Mr. Presley, you can help me." She scooted away from him and headed in the opposite direction. "I need you to reach something for me, if you please?"

Noah let her lead the way and could only imagine he resembled a dutiful pup following after his master. But in this instance, he made sure he walked far enough behind her that he didn't step on the hem of her ruffled skirt.

He also couldn't help but notice anytime Abigail entered the mercantile, her presence turned his mind to mush. His tongue stuck to the roof of his mouth, and what came out didn't resemble words in the King's English.

"Mr. Presley, ah, Mama's in need of some, ah, let me see. There it is." Abigail pointed up at the next to the top shelf at a row of kerosene bottles. "The hurricane lamps she unwrapped today need oil."

Noah nodded and stepped up on the ladder to retrieve the merchandise. He wondered why it had taken her mother so long to unpack her lamps. Night had fallen more than once since their arrival. If he'd known, he'd have taken some to them the day he went to call.

He reached his long arms up as high as they would go, but he still couldn't reach the bottles. Noah needed to talk to Adam about his placement of certain items. Top shelves. A location which required a ladder.

Help me, Jesus!

Taking another step up meant he would venture into uncharted territory, an area he let his brother navigate. The young man never batted an eye at heights, getting higher than the third rung on a ladder made Noah want to lose his lunch.

"Are we having a problem, Mr. Presley?"

"Heaven's no. I'll have it. . ." Noah took a downward glance at Abigail and immediately wished he hadn't. The wooden floor started to spin and he placed a death grip on the sides of the ladder to keep from falling from his perch.

"Are you sure you're all right?"

"I. . .I. . .I'm fine." Noah descended the steps as fast as he could, planting his two feet on the ground and praising the Lord when he landed on the planked flooring. "I'll see if there are any bottles in the back of the store."

He stepped behind the curtain, not waiting for Abigail to agree or disagree with his decision to do so. Sweat dripped off his forehead onto his faded denim apron, and his breathing came in short spurts.

Noah took his white handkerchief out of his back pocket, and wiped his face off, and made a mental note to have that talk with Adam sooner than later. He took a moment to calm down then found two bottles of kerosene on the middle shelf in the backroom.

He grabbed the items Miss Thompson wanted and was about ready to draw the curtain back when he heard the front door open. A second later, Abigail gasped.

Noah rushed out and his eyes beheld Otto Thompson, who stood inside the door of the mercantile. He held his hat in one hand and a silver pie tin in the other.

"Good afternoon, Mr. Thomp—"

"Papa, what are you doing here? Why aren't you in court?"

"Well, hello to you, too. Guess I could ask you the same question, but I already know the answer." Her papa gave Abigail a sideways glance. "And, if you must know, I came over to compliment Noah and tell him how much we enjoyed the pie." The older man handed Noah the tin.

"I'm glad you liked it. How about a cup of fresh coffee?" Noah strolled over to the counter and poured some beans into the grinder.

"Sounds good." Otto reached into his vest pocket and looked at his watch. "So, daughter, I gather the reason you're over here is you're hiding from your mama again?"

"Heavens no, Papa. I finished music lessons an hour ago. I came over here for …uh…some things."

"Mr. Thompson, she came in for—"

"Material, Papa. I came in to look at the material." Abigail patted the gingham check and seersucker fabric while keeping an eye on Noah.

"Miss Thompson?" Noah pointed to the back of the store. "You came in for—"

"This fabric, Mr. Presley."

Noah knew Abigail stopped him before he could disclose her unnecessary purchase. He watched her grab the colorful bolt of yellow check and head to the counter, pushing the yardage in his direction.

The silence surrounding Abigail spoke volumes. She glanced at the two men and neither wore a smile. Her cheeks immediately felt hot. Never before had she been so unladylike, interrupting a gentleman three times in less than two minutes.

Abigail took a deep breath and said, "I need two yards,

please."

Noah took the material and cut the amount she asked for. He wrapped it up in tissue paper and put the package to the side of the cash register. "Anything else, Miss?"

"No!"

Embarrassment clung to her like the cape draped across her petite shoulders. She eyed Noah as he walked over and finished preparing the coffee. The front door swung open again, announcing another customer.

"Noah, how's the coffee coming?" an older gentleman called out from the doorway. "It's smellin' mighty good today."

Abigail almost waltzed over and gave the fella a kiss on the cheek. He'd come in at just the right moment before another superfluous statement could tumble out of her lips.

"Gentlemen, have a seat. Coffee's just about ready." Noah motioned for them to sit.

"If you don't mind, I'll be over here looking at the seed catalogs."

"That's fine, Samuel." Noah readied two mugs and turned back to Abby's father. "Sir, how is Mrs. Thompson? Haven't seen her in town for a few days."

"Mama? Oh, she's too busy with my music." Abigail stopped midsentence when all three men set their eyes upon her.

Did those words just spill out of my mouth? Oh Lord, please save me now.

Papa shot a look in her direction, telling her he'd heard the words she'd intended for only herself. And, she'd better curb her sassiness. After a sip of coffee, he looked over at Noah. "Mrs. Thompson is doing just fine. But, I'm sure she still misses her friends back in Dallas."

"I bet she does. Central City is quite a change from Texas." Samuel Collins came over to the counter and sat down.

"Yes, it is, but I know when the opera house gets fixed up, Ivy will be fit as a fiddle."

Abigail watched Noah. Again the color drained from his face. He fiddled with the lid on the candy jar, but it seemed to not want to open.

"Sir, I'm not sure what Pop's going to do." Noah finished unscrewing the lid and held it in his hand. "Right now he's in Denver looking at some pla—"

"No, I'm not. I got back this afternoon."

The gentleman's booming voice made Abigail jump to the side of the counter. She also noticed Noah almost flung the lid he held across the room when the older man stepped from behind the curtain at the back of the mercantile.

"And, speaking of which, have you seen my invoice book?"

"Your. . .your book?" Noah stumbled over the two words and looked like he'd bit into a lemon.

"Yeah. My ledger."

"Haven't seen it, Pop, and anyway I thought the meeting with the opera board wasn't until Monday."

"Didn't want to wait two more days. Them Denver people are a bunch of stuffed shirts. Don't need 'em for what I want to do. Had to get back to talk to the banker. It couldn't wait." Noah's father turned and headed to the back of the store.

"Well, Mr. Presley, for my wife's sake I hope your plans include redoing the place."

The man stopped and spun around to stare at Abby's father. Noah seemed to sense trouble brewing, along with the coffee. He stepped toward his father and said, "Pop, I don't know where my manners are. I'd like you to meet the newest residents of Central City. Mr. Otto Thompson and his daughter, Miss Abigail Thompson."

"Pleased to meet you, Miss." Cyrus tipped his hat in Abigail's direction, his expression softening some. Then he looked at her father before he said, "Mr. Thompson, I'm not sure I'm going to reopen the opera house. Don't know yet." Without so much as another word he turned back around and walked to the curtain and opened it then disappeared behind its folds.

The slamming of a door told Abigail that Cyrus Presley exited the mercantile and was not too happy. His leaving rattled the inside of the wooden structure.

"Would you two gentlemen like a refill?" Noah's question filled the awkward silence Cyrus left behind.

"Nah. Gotta be gettin' back to the office." Samuel Collins stood up and grabbed his cap as he headed to the front door. He stopped. "Noah, if I know your father he's probably going to turn the dilapidated place into a gambling hall." Samuel laughed as he left the mercantile.

Even from across the room Abigail saw the sadness in the store owner's eyes. She could only imagine his troubled thoughts. Would his father really turn the famed opera house into a den of thieves? Abby's stomach did a complete somersault as she ventured down that road.

"Noah, your father wouldn't think of opening such an establishment? Would he?" Again Abigail blurted out her thoughts before she had time to think them through. Her face suddenly felt very warm and grew even hotter when she realized she'd called the store owner by his first name.

Four

Noah watched Mr. Thompson and Abigail cross the cobblestone street after they left the mercantile. He still couldn't figure out why Miss Thompson had come in and why she didn't want the bottles of kerosene after he'd almost killed himself getting them for her.

There's something odd about Abigail, but I do have to say she's a lovely distraction.

Not that Noah had time to clutter his mind with the female's peculiarities. His father's unexpected return to Central City caused him enough problems, never mind the fact that he'd lied to him about the whereabouts of his ledger. The one he had hidden under the counter.

"Yes, Pop, I've got your ledger and I'm going to keep it. For the time being. One entry looks interesting." Noah's words echoed in the empty mercantile and the sound of his boots resonated on the wooden floor as he made his way across the store.

He walked by the table of material and his eyes caught sight of the mess Miss Thompson had made of the summer cottons. He straightened the bolts of fabric. His thoughts went again to the young woman. Immediately, his heart beat a little faster.

Noah took a deep breath to calm himself down and hoped to clear his mind of the spirited nineteen-year old.

Lord, I don't have time to think about her.

More important things commanded Noah's attention—namely the Central City Opera House. The place his grandparents owned and where he'd spent most of his childhood. After school he'd go there to hear his mother and grandmother rehearse for its next show. Gram would always have him practice his piano lessons after they finished.

Noah wanted nothing more than to purchase and restore the opera house to its original finery that he remembered. The thought of his father turning the place into a gambling hall caused his blood to boil and he shouted, "Pop, I don't know what I'm going to do, but a brothel isn't going to happen. Not if I can help it."

Movement outside the mercantile caught Noah's attention. Jake Taylor, the banker, crossed Main Street, heading towards the Teller House. A sudden urge for meatloaf overpowered his senses. Noah made a decision as he turned the *Closed* sign over to face the street. First time in Presley Mercantile history, he closed the store at 2:30 in the afternoon.

Noah didn't have much dealings with the banker. His pop trusted him, but for some reason he had never done any business with Jake. However, in this case, the older man might be convinced to talk his father into selling the opera house.

"Mr. Taylor, all I'm saying is I have plenty of money."

Noah scooped up a fork full of mashed potatoes. Instead of putting the utensil into his mouth, he pointed it at the banker who sat across from him at the Teller House.

"Son, you've told me this a hundred times. At least. As I've said before, I'm not the one you need to talk to." The gray haired man lifted his coffee cup in the air. Mollie strolled over and refilled it. "Thanks, darling."

"You two need anything else?"

"Yes, we do. Bring Jake and me a piece of your world-famous apple pie," Noah spoke for both of them. He knew the longer he kept the man there, the more questions he could ask him.

"Trying to fatten me up ain't goin' to get any more answers out of me," Jake Taylor commented as he yanked the napkin off his lap and tucked the end of it under the collar of his oxford shirt.

"No, but I can keep you here for a few more minutes. Just in case." Noah chuckled and finished his biscuit after he dipped it in the last of the creamed gravy on his plate.

"Son, I cannot, in good conscience, disclose information about your father's business. Anyway, there's a chance he has someone interested in the opera house already. He's waiting for the pap—"

The banker stopped. His sudden silence enveloped the occupants of the square table. Noah let the man's words sink in, and then asked, "Who did he sell it to?" The clatter of pans in the kitchen drowned out the end of his question.

"None of your concern. Shouldn't have said anything." Jake Taylor tore the napkin from his collar and stood. "Son, talk to your father." The banker threw a token on the table and left. Noah sat alone staring at the two pieces of apple pie Mollie Blair had set in front of him.

The door of the yellow Victorian slammed behind Abigail on her way to escape another music lesson. She froze in place on the porch, hoping her mama hadn't heard the racket her exit made. Heavy footsteps in the foyer informed her that she'd been found out.

"Abigail Jane Thompson, get yourself back in he—"

She didn't wait to hear anything else. Freedom yelled louder than her mother. Abigail ran as hard as her legs would carry her, right smack dab into her papa coming up the brick walkway.

"Daughter, don't you think your running from your music lessons is getting a bit out of hand?" Her father questioned her as he glanced down at his disheveled Stetson hat. From all accounts it sustained a slight injury in their collision.

"Oh, Papa, I'm so sorry. Here let me straighten it for you." Abigail took his hat and while she smoothed out the extra crease she'd help create she said, "But, Papa, she can't make me sing a solo. I don't care if it's Homecoming Sunday."

"Now, now. How about we take the horses out for a ride? We haven't been out for a while since the weather's turned chilly." He smothered a cough.

"Are you sure?" The very idea made her fret. "Papa, this north wind might not be good on your cold."

"I'll be just fine. You go on ahead and I'll go tell Mama what we're doing. Don't want her calling the sheriff out on you." He laughed out loud, which triggered another coughing fit.

"Papa?"

"Don't you worry, dear." He caught a little gasp of air.

"I'm fine. Get going."

"Thanks." Abigail leaned closer to her papa, making sure she missed his Stetson this time, and gave him a kiss on the cheek before she high-tailed herself the few blocks to the livery stable.

On her way down the cobblestone walkway, the wind whipped her corduroy skirt around her high top boots. The folds of the material almost made her trip. Abigail stopped and straightened her bothersome skirt. "One day, Lord, and please make it soon, I hope someone designs something less cumbersome for a woman to wear."

Abigail continued on her way, sidestepping a puddle or two, and decided she must find a pair of Papa's pants when she got home that evening. But first things first. Abby rounded the corner and heard Herkimer whinny. His greeting when he saw her.

She often told people she thought her horse smiled when he saw her coming. Dancer, her papa's horse, on the other hand, stood tall and regal in the last stall. He waited patiently to do his master's bidding. His satin black coat glistened in the afternoon glow of the sun.

"Missy, let me help you with those." Mr. Price hefted Dancer's saddle and tossed it up on the large animal. "No need for you to hurt yourself," he assured her. Abigail appreciated the owner's help, even though she could do the task herself. She usually stepped up on a hay bale. The extra height did wonders for her ability to get the two horses saddled without Mr. Price's assistance.

She grabbed Dancer and Herkimer's reins and led them back home. Her papa waited for her on their expansive porch, posed and ready for their outing. Mama stood next to him and looked none too happy with either one of them.

Abby's Mama turned and said something to Papa as he headed off the porch. He nodded and tipped his hat in her mother's direction.

"Abigail, you make sure your papa keeps that scarf tied around his neck." She smiled while she brought her pink sweater closer around her shoulders, buttoning the top pearl button at her neck.

"Okay, Mama. I don't want his cold to get worse, either." Abby climbed up on Herkimer and steadied him with her gentle touch.

"Have a good time," Mama said as she opened the screen door.

Abigail and her father rode down Main Street and as they neared the corner, Noah came out of the Teller House. Her heart leapt at the sight of the handsome Mr. Presley.

"Good afternoon." Abigail smiled at Noah, hoping he'd return the favor. She wanted to see his cute dimple.

"Afternoon." Noah crossed the street with not another word spoken. He then disappeared into the mercantile.

Abby struggled to understand his disinterested response. After a moment she glanced her father's way. "Papa, I'm not too sure, but I think something's going on with Mr. Presley. Did you see how he reacted when his father dropped in on him the other day?"

"Sure did. And whatever happened in the Teller House today didn't help matters." Papa pointed back over his shoulder at the young man.

Abigail nodded as they made their way down Main Street, her mood not as festive after their encounter with Noah. She didn't know why his one-word response bothered her so much. In the short time she'd lived in Central City he'd never talked her ear off, but his brusque reply today surprised her. And, in the end, she didn't get to see his smile and his dimple stayed hidden under a mystery only he knew about.

"Daughter, why are you frowning?"

"Hmm?" Abby startled to attention. Not wanting to share her thoughts, she decided to change the subject. "Papa, say we forget Mr. Presley and get some riding done. I'll race you to Digger's Gulch."

She didn't wait for an answer. Abigail took off as fast as Herkimer would carry her. All she had to do was hold on tight to the reins. No need to worry about falling from her saddle now, she and her beloved mare knew the trails and twists and turns around Central City and Black Hawk. The faster they went, the more the crisp September air bit at her cheeks.

Digger's Gulch loomed in the distance. The tiny cemetery at the edge of the ravine warned unsuspecting visitors of the impending valley on the other side. Abigail slowed Herkimer down and glanced over her shoulder, wanting to see how substantially she'd beat her papa.

Instead of basking in sure victory, Abby whipped her horse around and raced back to her father. Dancer stood still while her father tried desperately to catch his breath. Papa slumped over the saddle gasping for air.

"Papa?" She screamed as she jumped off her horse and ran over to him. "Papa?"

"I. . .I. . ." His words disappeared into another coughing fit. Her father's face turned crimson as he gasped for breath and his lips appeared somewhat off-color. Or was that just her imagination?

Abigail grabbed the canteen off Herkimer and shoved it into her father's hand. "Please, Papa, drink some of this." She didn't know what else to do. "You're winded."

"Y-yes." He gripped the canteen and managed to take a

drink of water. The gasping seemed to slow after a few minutes, replaced by a soft wheezing noise, which sounded something akin to the whistling wind.

Papa took a couple of more sips and before long the color in his lips returned and his crimson cheeks dulled to their usual color. He glanced Abigail's way and his brows arched. "Daughter, don't give me that look. I'm fine." As he passed the canteen her way, she couldn't help but notice the trembling in his hands.

"Papa, you aren't either fine. That was the worst episode yet. And your voice is raspier. You're not fooling me one second. I think it's time we turn around and went home. Get you in where it's warm." Abigail bossed as she got back on her horse and headed west.

"Yes Ma'am." He gave her a little salute.

She kept Herkimer close to Dancer all the way back into town. The rattling sound she heard every time her father took a breath concerned her. *Could it be pneumonia? Oh, Lord, please help Papa.*

Her mama must have seen them coming down Main because she rushed down off the porch and helped him down off the saddle.

"He had a bad spell out there, Mama." Abigail's voice quivered as she spoke. She knew she needed to stay strong, but right then she wanted to stand in their front yard and sob.

"Take the horses, Abby. On your way back, stop and get Doc Stanton. Your papa needs some medicine."

Abigail rushed back to the livery stable. Mr. Price gave her a quizzical look. "Something the matter, miss?"

"Papa's not doing well. Can you please put Herkimer and Dancer up for me?"

"Sure. Don't you worry now."

Abigail ran the short distance to the doctor's office. The kerosene lights inside illuminated the light dusting of snow on his porch. She flung open the door and not waiting for the older man to acknowledge her, she yelled. "Doc, can you come help Papa?"

He spun his chair around. "Dear, what's the problem?" He got up and walked the few steps to the door and closed it.

"No, sir, you need to come now." She took a hold of his sleeve and pulled on it. Never in her life had she done something so audacious, but this was her papa.

"Let me get my bag." Doc Stanton looked inside and took something off one of his shelves and they headed over to Main Street.

For the next half hour, Abigail and her mama prayed and paced the parlor floor. Abigail knew the Lord held her Papa's life in His mighty hands and for sure would never let anything happen to him. Hadn't they just started a brand new life in Colorado? Her papa would be just fine. Nary a doubt clouded her mind.

Finally, Abigail sat down on the burgundy settee in the parlor. Her feet inside her laced up boots hurt. She wanted to take them off, but she didn't want to do two unladylike gestures in one afternoon.

To keep her hands busy, she traced the intricate pattern on the material of the fainting couch with her index finger. Each delicate curved line curled to touch the next, holding on to the other, never letting go. *So much like our family. Oh, Lord, Papa has to be alright.*

The bedroom door closed. Doc Stanton stood at the parlor door. His brow furrowed, but his eyes smiled at them.

"Mrs. Thompson, I gave Otto something to help him rest. He should sleep through the night. That's what he really needs.

I left a tin with a few more pills inside. He'll be fine in a few days."

"Thank you. We appreciate you coming on such short notice."

"No problem, Mrs. Thompson. Honestly, I'm not sure your daughter would have let go of me if I hadn't."

The doctor laughed heartily, but what held Abigail's attention was her mama, who gave her a sidelong glance. The same look her father would have given her, if he'd been able to.

No doubt Abigail's cheeks turned a deep shade of red with his announcement and her forthrightness. But she wasn't concerned. Doc said her papa would get well in short order. *Thank You, Lord. I knew he'd be okay.*

Five

"How's Papa's cough this morning?" Abigail asked her mama as they headed down the stairs.

"A little better, but—"

"Daughter, what your mama's saying is I'm doing better for only being on the awful medicine Doc Stanton gave me a week ago," Papa's voice rang out from inside the master bedroom.

Abigail strolled over and peeked around the door jamb into her parent's room. Her father sat on the edge of the bed. She watched him wipe his forehead with his handkerchief. That gesture, coupled with his still pale features, worried her but she kept her concerns to herself.

"Well, Papa, you best be getting better. It's lonely riding out there by myself."

"Why don't you saddle up Dancer?" He gave her a playful wink. "I'm raring to go."

"Otto Thompson, my stars, you'll do no such thing," Mama's voice almost shook the bedroom window panes when she came up and stood next to Abigail. "That rattling in your chest has still got me concerned."

"Darlin' it's nothing. Now go fix me some of that putrid tea the doc prescribed. If it doesn't kill me, it might just cure me."

Her mama turned and started to descend the long staircase mumbling under her breath. Abigail followed her after she stopped to blow a kiss to her papa.

"He better drink this tea instead of that coffee over at Presley Mercantile." Mama continued her grumbling. "I'm not sure he should have gone out yesterday, but he insisted."

Yes, Abigail remembered and would have gone along with her papa, but her mother had other ideas. Her daughter must rehearse for her solo on Homecoming Sunday.

Abby sang all four verses of the sacred hymn the day before. In between each verse she'd ask when her mama planned on giving her friend, Mollie Blair, singing lessons. No answer came.

"So, Abigail, since your papa is feeling better today, and won't mind a little noise, why don't you hurry on over and get Mollie?" Mama's words brought her back to the kitchen, but what her mother said next made Abby want to give her mother a kiss.

"Daughter, I know she's anxious for me to begin her music lessons. Not to mention someone else I know who's been pestering me about it."

Before her mama could change her mind, Abigail rushed out the front door and down the steps. She was biting at the bit for her friend to get busy on her lessons. If Mollie was going to take her place on Homecoming Sunday, her mama must get busy. Mollie Blair needed all the assistance her mother could give her. And, Abigail wasn't sure there was anything or anybody in the whole state of Colorado to get that girl singing on key.

While Mollie Blair more than enthusiastically tried to master the art of singing, Abigail opened her Bible. She figured it couldn't hurt to pray for her friend. Or in her case, plead with her Heavenly Father to send the miracle she desired at that very moment.

"Miss Blair, I don't believe the Good Lord intended Middle C to sound quite that interesting." Abigail's mother tapped her stick lightly on the music stand. "Now, let's try it one more time, shall we?"

Abigail watched her mama direct her friend's singing voice up and down the scales. She had to cover her mouth before laughter spilled out of both sides of it. Mollie Blair truly could not sing her way out of anything.

This news had already traveled through all the circles of The Baptist Church of Central City, but Abigail Thompson didn't give a hoot that Mollie couldn't sing. The more time her mama spent teaching her new best friend, meant less practicing for herself.

Since the day Abigail and Mollie met at church, she'd told Abby she wanted to sing professionally. Her expression today spoke of the sheer determination to do so or die trying. When she found out Abby didn't want to sing on Homecoming Sunday, Mollie said, "Step aside. I'll take your place."

The only problem with this proposition, clergy and parishioners from years gone by would attend this much anticipated event. The special program committee wanted everything perfect—not someone who was tone deaf to the tips of her toes.

"I do believe we've had enough for one day," Abby's mother finally said as she laid her baton on the grand piano. She cleared her throat and looked directly at Mollie. Abigail imagined Mama was doing her best to choose her next words carefully, not blurting something out without reason or thought.

"Miss Blair. . .uh. . .before we set up another. . .singing lesson, I'd like to speak to your mother." The pitch of her mama's voice rose higher with each syllable spoken.

"Oh, Mrs. Thompson, Mother would be pleased to chat." Mollie's cheeks glowed pink. She clasped her hands together in obvious glee. "She was so excited when you agreed to give me lessons. You simply have no idea. Why, she places so much stock in your skills as an instructor. My mama simply can't wait to see the results of your labors."

Abby couldn't wait, either. She listened while Mollie continued to give her mother compliment after compliment. She didn't have the heart to tell her friend that her teacher hadn't agreed without there being many reservations.

After a moment of silence Mama said, "Proper singing requires extensive training. Hours of work, going over your scales, fine-tuning your pitch, training your ear."

"I've never been afraid of hard work." Mollie's lips turned up in a bright smile. "But remember, Mrs. Thompson, I work some evenings at the Teller House. I'm saving for college next year. I hope to major in music at one of the schools back East. And writing your name on my application will put a feather in my bonnet with the faculty, I'm sure." Mollie Blair didn't have a clue she'd just helped her cause with such glowing accolades.

"And my mama is here to help, Mollie, anytime. Anyway

she can."

Abigail's mother let out an exasperated sigh as she picked the baton up off the piano. She began to tap it on the palm of her hand. Abby counted fifteen times. Again, she knew her mother worked at trying to think how to respond tactfully.

While she searched for the right words to say, Abby prayed silently, "Lord, please tell Mama to let Mollie come for more lessons. It's sure to benefit all of us in the end. Amen!"

"Good morning, Mrs. Collins. How are you on this chilly October morning?" Noah Presley poured the town's gossip a cup of his world famous coffee. He wondered what 'news' she'd have to share with him today.

"Son, I'm fair to middlin'. Thanks for asking. That cough I've had is still giving me a heap of trouble, but thank goodness I'm doing better than Otto Thompson. Heard he's knocking at death's door."

"Mrs. Collins, I beg your pardon?" Noah hoped his question didn't give away his displeasure at her outlandish statement.

"I'm just telling you what I heard." Edna Mae Collins tugged at the sleeve of her jacket. "And, that's why I thought it a tad strange when I saw the Blair girl go into their house. Saw her when I headed over here this morning. I assume she's going to her music lesson. If I were her mother, I'm not too sure I'd have allowed her to go in that infected home. Doc Stanton should quarantine the place. That's what I think."

Noah only half-listened to her. As most times, the woman didn't have a clue who or what she was talking about. Especially today, giving him, and heaven knew who else, Mr.

Thompson's diagnosis as forthright as she did. The man had been in the mercantile the day before and said he felt much better. 'A few days in bed cures most ills,' he'd told him.

"And her voice is that of an angel."

"I'm sorry. Who are we talking about? Were you saying that Mollie has the voice of an angel?" Noah couldn't imagine anyone thinking the young woman's voice sounded like it came from up above. "Mrs. Collins, you must be talking about someone else entirely." Noah suppressed a laugh.

"I am, or I should say Mollie is telling everyone that *Abigail* sounds like a choir of angels when she raises her voice to the Lord."

"Oh, my yes, Mrs. Collins, I couldn't agree more." Noah knew he showed a little too much enthusiasm on the subject at hand. Instantly, he hoped his zeal didn't make the older woman start rumors about him and Miss Thompson.

But Noah couldn't help smiling when he remembered hearing Abigail's voice the day he took the apple pie over to welcome the Thompsons to town. He'd never heard a sweeter sound coming from a parlor in all his years. Gram Presley, God rest her soul, would be honored to come back from heaven to hear the young woman sing a hymn or two.

"And, Mr. Presley," Mrs. Collins leaned over the counter and whispered. "I heard another bit of news. Come Homecoming Sunday, Miss Abigail Thompson is going to sing a solo for us. That's if she doesn't find a way out of it. Then Mollie will take her place."

"What in the world are you talking about?"

"Mr. Noah Presley, settle yourself down, and don't be giving me that look of yours. I'm just telling you what *they* told me." The older woman backed away from the counter. Noah noticed she wore a satisfied smile on her weathered face as she turned around to check out the fabric table.

She left him to wonder who 'they' were, but Noah didn't ask. He wasn't in the mood for another long-winded explanation. He finished wiping up around the coffee pot, and then went over and rang up Mrs. Collins's purchases. When the bell over the door finally chimed, he knew Mrs. Tittle-Tattle had left the mercantile.

Thank goodness. Now where is that brother of mine? Adam said he'd be here to help me stock the shelves.

Abigail almost ran over and gave her mama a kiss. She'd agreed to let Mollie come back for another lesson on Friday. But as delighted as this news made Abby, she knew there was still a lot of work to do. Mollie Blair would never be able to master any singing talent if Mama quit all her practices at twenty-five minutes, instead of the usual hour or so.

Fear began to weigh heavy on Abby's heart. The jitters jumping up inside her every time she thought of singing anywhere made her think about feigning an ailment. What would it hurt? Pretend a little sore throat a few days before Homecoming Sunday. Come the morning of the big celebration, she could have a full-blown malady.

She'd be home free and not have to sing a note. Mollie would have the limelight, something her friend desired with all her heart, soul, mind and strength.

"Lord, maybe just this once," she whispered. "Please. No one would know but the two of us. I can keep a secret. I promise I won't tell a soul what I did."

But what she'd learned in Sunday school and her parent's teaching her the golden rule told Abigail that telling a lie wouldn't work. Anyway, her mama could read through her plan like an open book on a windy day.

Abigail needed to do something to calm herself down and she knew what would do the trick. Her horse, Herkimer, would help her to think clearer so she could come up with another option. But first, she had to run upstairs and change into something a little more comfortable.

About a half mile out of town, Abigail stopped her horse and slid off his side. "Herkimer, I need to talk to you and it's important. We're going to try something different and you'll have to relax."

Abigail stroked Herkimer's neck as she continued to chatter. "Trying to ride you like Papa does Dancer is gonna seem strange to both of us for a while, but I know we can do this. Today I need to ride and sort out some things and I can't do it hanging on to you for dear life."

She glanced toward the mining town, making sure nobody would witness her high jinx. And as she did, she caught sight of the snow-covered peaks around her new home. Their beauty embraced her.

Abigail drank in the stillness until Herkimer jostled her, making her trip. "Whoa, boy." Abigail decided she'd better quit daydreaming and get to riding. She put her left foot in the stirrup and pulled herself up and swung her right leg over her horse's back.

Since she'd worn her 'borrowed' pair of trousers from Papa, no worries about displaying more than the law allowed a woman to show. Once settled into the saddle, she and Herkimer took off heading north.

The freedom Abigail felt riding this new and unfamiliar way sent chills running through every part of her being. The jumbled thoughts from earlier evaporated into midair as she drank in the beauty surrounding her.

Abigail brought her horse to a slow gallop as they neared Digger's Gulch. Without having to touch his reins, Herkimer came to a stop a couple of feet from the edge. Abby got off and stared at the mountains, hoping they'd give her the answers she sought.

They didn't, but the verses she'd read in Proverbs that morning rang in her head. *Trust in the Lord with all thine heart, and lean not unto thine own understanding. In all thy ways acknowledge him, and he shall direct thy paths.*

"Lord, I'm not sure what Your plans are, but I hope and pray they don't include me having to get up and sing."

Six

Noah quit sweeping the mercantile when his eyes caught sight of his baby brother. He couldn't help but throw a barb or two his way. "Adam Presley, are you going to get yourself in here? You told me the day before yesterday I could count on you helping me stock the shelves."

"Noah, keep your trousers on. The supplies ain't going anywhere." The younger Presley side stepped the jars of pickles stacked on the wood floor.

"Trust me, a man who don't keep his word is the devil's. . ." Noah left his preachy retort hanging in the air. No need to stir up trouble with his sibling, even if he wanted to choke him at that very moment. Noah reasoned that if he caused his brother's demise, there'd be no one else willing to climb up the rickety ladder and stock the higher shelves in the mercantile.

"Is climbing up this thing all I'm good for?" Adam chuckled as he pointed to the wooden ladder a few feet away from them.

"For the moment, I'd have to say yes." And for the life of him, Noah couldn't find another use for Adam 'cause he never hung around long enough to find any other good reason for him to be at the mercantile. He always found an excuse to hang around their father and all his other 'businesses.'

Adam waltzed by Noah on his way to the ladder. He tipped his hat with one hand. With the other he took a jab at Noah's ribs. This caused the two of them to exchange words, but finally the younger Presley hauled the case of pickle jars up the five rungs and placed each jar on the topmost shelf.

"There. Are you happy?" Adam asked, still perched high on the ladder.

"Ecstatic." Noah stopped at the one-word answer. He wanted to add more but the bell on the mercantile door alerted him they had a customer. He turned to extend a greeting to whoever it may be. He smiled when he recognized a familiar face.

"Good morning, Samuel."

"Good morning, to you as well. Hey, Noah, I see you got someone doing that high up work for ya again. When are you going to get over your fear of heights?"

Adam bounced off the last step, landing on the floor with a thud. "Mr. Collins, I hope he gets over it soon. I got better things to do than hang out in this boring place."

"Son, I'll bet you do. I'll bet you do. And knowing your pop like I do, it sounds like you two are cut out of the same cloth." Samuel strolled over and grabbed a stool from against the wall and sat down at the counter.

Noah couldn't have agreed more with Samuel's assessment of his brother, but kept it to himself. Only by the grace of God. He could almost feel the Lord holding his tongue so as not to say words he'd regret later. *Adam, you and me are goin' have a long talk. You can count on it.*

"Mr. Collins, how about that cup of coffee my brother offered you?" Adam elbowed past Noah and grabbed the coffee pot, pouring Samuel a cup out of the freshly brewed pot.

"Son, you read my mind. Noah's coffee is the reason I come in this place, and to see what you two boys are up to." The older man took a couple of swigs of his hot coffee, and then held it up for a refill. His toothless grin appeared after he wiped his mouth with the back of his hand.

Noah let Samuel's comments slide. He knew the owner of the telegraph office didn't come in to snoop on he and Adam. Unlikely, but he certainly wasn't going to give the man anything he could run home and tell his wife, Mrs. Collins—Central City's town gossip.

"Mr. Collins, let me fill 'er up for you, and then I need to scoot." Adam retrieved the pot and topped off the old man's coffee cup.

"Where you heading, son?"

"Me, Pop and Matthew Tappen are meeting the banker for some kind of meeting. Big plans are in the works."

"Matthew Tappen? Never heard of him." Samuel pushed himself back on his three-legged stool.

Noah couldn't help but wonder, himself. "Yeah, who is he? I've been hearing a lot about this guy from Pop." *And reading about him in his ledger.*

Adam offered a little shrug. "Mr. Tappen's the lumberman from Idaho Springs. He's pretty interested in helping Pop fix up the opera house."

"Last I heard, your father was selling." Mr. Collins quirked a brow.

"Nah. Pop ain't getting rid of the old place." Adam

headed to the front door and turned around and looked at Noah. "I'll see you later." He headed out the front door before Noah could object to his leaving.

"Fine, just leave. No problem," Noah announced as he walked over and looked out the window. "Adam, Pop's got you bamboozled. You, as well as me, know his big plans are to find some fool to bail him out again. And, if I wasn't so scared to talk to him, I could be the person he's looking for."

"Son, what in tarnation?"

Noah spun around and faced Samuel Collins. "Oh my stars, you scared me half to death. I forgot you were still here."

"You don't say." Samuel laughed. "Now son, are you going to tell me what you were mumbling about?"

Noah had no intention of telling anyone anything, especially the husband of the town's tell-everything-she-hears busybody. He couldn't believe what he'd blurted out. In just fifteen minutes the owner of the telegraph office had been in the store, he already had plenty to tell his wife. Noah wasn't going to add any more to the juicy tidbits.

"Now, Mr. Collins, how about some more of my delicious coffee?" Noah hummed *Amazing Grace* as he poured his friend another cup.

"Otto Thompson, get yourself in here this minute. You're still ailing."

As Mama shouted out of the back screen, Abigail almost poked herself with the end of the paring knife. *I wish she'd warn me before she goes and does that. Give me time to prepare.*

Abby guessed by her mama's reaction she must have

spied Papa crossing Main Street and wanted to hurry him inside their toasty home. The evening fire raged in the stone fireplace, while the north wind howled outside the kitchen window.

The late October snow continued to fall, blanketing the tiny mining town of Central City, Colorado. For sure, her Papa didn't need to be out in this inclement weather, especially since the nasty cough he'd caught close to a month before persisted.

"Ivy, will you hush or our neighbors will wonder who's getting murdered over here." Papa laughed as he shook the white flakes off his wool coat and Stetson hat. He hung his garments on the hook near the pantry, and then turned and gave his wife a hug and peck on the cheek.

She shooed away his kisses. "Mr. Thompson, you'll do well to keep away from your daughter and me. You don't want us coming down with any of this, do you?"

"Heavens, no. Wouldn't want to share this with anyone," Papa answered, his voice sounding a bit deeper than normal.

"Maybe if you did, you'd get done with it a little faster," Abby added with a chuckle. "Then you and I could do some riding. I don't know about you, but I'm missin' our jaunts out into the Rocky Mountains."

"Indeed, daughter." He reached over the counter and took a slice of potato off the pile in front of Abby.

"My dear, you or your papa will do no such thing." Mama stopped and raised her hand to her mouth. The gesture stopped her impending lecture, but did nothing to curb a bit of laughter, which escaped behind her cupped hand. "Otto, you'll do yourself well if you quit looking at me like that. Those sad eyes of yours aren't going to work this time."

Even if her papa didn't feel up to par, he could still get her and Mama to laugh. Abigail smiled at her parents and silently prayed she'd know that kind of love in her own heart one day. Immediately, her thoughts drifted to Noah Presley, the owner of the local mercantile. *Goodness sakes, what has come over me?*

She tried to put the image of him and his adorable dimple out of her head, but nothing short of moving to a foreign country could stop her from thinking about this interesting young man.

"Dear, are we going to have those potatoes done tonight or next Thursday?" Mama turned and started tapping her foot on the wood floor.

"Sorry." Abby stood up straighter and put her hands back to the chore of peeling. Again, her thoughts returned to Noah. She smiled and started humming. Why on earth she picked the hymn her mama expected her to sing in a few weeks was beyond her. She knew she wasn't going to sing. No way, no how. *Lord, I need a divine inter—no, actually, I need a miracle. Mollie Blair has to learn how to sing before November fourth.*

"Pop, how about selling me the opera house, instead of JAR Corp.?" Noah practiced the line in front of his shaving mirror Sunday morning before leaving for church. The question sounded lame when it came out of his mouth.

And as he spoke the words, the usual apprehension gripped his insides when he thought about asking his father anything. Noah brushed off his suit jacket and glanced at his reflection again. "Oh, while I'm at it, why don't I ask him about his new friend Matthew Tappen, too."

As Noah slipped into his top coat on his way out the backdoor, he could almost hear his father's laughter and quick response, "Don't think that's none of your business, son."

"But, Pop, it did become my business when someone, other than family, is making decisions concerning the opera house and I'm not sure who the somebody is." Noah adjusted the scarf around his neck as he headed through the freshly fallen snow to The First Baptist Church at the top of the hill.

The early morning crispness should have cooled down Noah's dander, but it didn't. All it did was fuel the fire and brought him back to the problem at hand. Who and what was JAR Corporation and why were they trying to buy the opera house?

While Noah contemplated how he'd muster up the courage he needed to question his pop, something caused his attention to sway in a different direction. Miss Abigail Thompson came waltzing across the snow-covered street. Noah's heart seemed to change positions in his chest as he took in her beautiful face and winsome smile. He tugged at the front of his suit vest, hoping to realign it.

Suddenly, his thoughts concerning the opera house disappeared. Noah wondered where Abigail had kept herself the last week, but surmised it must have had to do with her father's illness. But what puzzled him even more than her not coming into the mercantile, he realized he'd missed her and her sassiness.

He watched as Abigail stepped gingerly up the stairs of the church. She held up her long woolen skirt, he assumed, so the hem didn't get dampened in the moisture on the steps. His eyes ventured down to her tiny ankle. He knew he shouldn't spy, but he couldn't help taking the opportunity God handed him on a silver platter. Noah almost gasped at what he thought he witnessed down by her boots. But could he be sure? No! Couldn't be that the young woman wore a pair of trousers under her fancy Sunday attire?

"Good morning, Mr. Presley. You look as if you've seen a ghost."

Noah nodded and try as he might, he couldn't think of a thing to say. He reasoned his lack of speech had to do with what he thought he saw under her skirt. *Oh my heavenly Father, that didn't come out right.*

He moved back a few steps and held the massive door for Abigail. She walked past him into the foyer of the church. He followed behind her, letting the door close behind him and her. All of a sudden traffic quit moving and she stopped right in front of him. Noah had to catch himself before he ran her over, again.

"Goodness me." Abigail turned and glanced up at Noah; her cheeks crimson red. "Oh, Mr. Presley, pardon me."

Noah still couldn't find words and he knew if he tried to say anything, he'd babble something foolish. He remembered the last time a near miss happened between the two of them. They'd been at the mercantile right after she'd moved to Central City. He still had the bottles of kerosene wrapped up in the back storeroom and would always wonder why she didn't want them.

Once the crowd dispersed, Abigail moved away from Noah. He did his best not to stare at her while she took off her knitted scarf. A few strands of her long blonde curls caught in the yarn causing them to pull out of the beaded clip at the nape of her neck. He knew at that moment his mouth hung wide open and if he didn't shut it soon anyone milling about would notice and tell him to shut his trap.

Noah closed his mouth and headed toward the double

doors. He kept an eye on Abigail as she entered the sanctuary, right behind her friend Mollie Blair. The two of them chatted as they took their seats. He sat a few rows back in the Presley pew. His pop and Adam decidedly absent.

He knew if Gram Presley were alive, she'd tan their hides for their sinful behavior of missing church. He also knew his grandmother would help him step up and do what the Lord intended him to do. To muster up the courage to talk to his father about selling the opera house to him, not someone else.

Seven

"Mollie Blair, in all my days, I've never heard a more dreadful singing voice. Furthermore…" The rest of her mother's sentence dangled in the air of the parlor on Thursday afternoon.

Every fiber of Abigail's being tensed up when she remembered her mama's unpleasant words directed at her friend's musical talent. Words that should have remained unspoken.

Mollie ran from the room with tears streaming down her cheeks. Abby wanted to chase after her and reprimand her mother all at the same time. Instead she shivered on the front porch, unable to go in either direction. Her leather boots seemed glued to the planks, holding her in place as she watched her friend disappear down the street. Never once looking back.

Chilled to the bone, Abigail finally turned and went back inside the house. Sadness enveloped her as she headed upstairs to change into her riding gear. Each step she took carried her closer to the real reason why her mama spoke so sharp to Mollie that day.

Her papa lay in bed, still feeling poorly. The grip of pneumonia still lingered, holding him in its clutches. Abigail noticed her papa's normal positive attitude disappeared with each racking cough. Concern etched her mama's face. It seemed she'd aged ten years in just a few short months.

She heard her mama's voice coming from her parents' room when she hit the top step. If she hadn't been in such a toot, she'd have eavesdropped on them. But she couldn't right then, Abigail needed to get out of the house. Take Herkimer out for a very long ride again. To think and pray, even if snow swirled around the second story windows as she looked out.

Today, a 'Come to Jesus' meeting would be on the agenda and it would happen as soon as she put on her papa's pants and headed out to Digger's Gulch, her favorite place to call out to her Lord and Savior.

"The hurrier you go, Abigail, the behinder you get," She spouted the saying her mama always used as the heel of her boot got caught in the hem of her papa's trousers. Twisting and tugging until her foot loosed from its one-legged trap almost caused her to topple over. With her footing restored, she maneuvered the other pant leg without so much as a hitch.

She paused to survey herself in the full-length mirror, making sure nothing peeked out from under the hem of her woolen skirt. Thoughts of Noah immediately snuck into her already harried mind. Abby could feel her cheeks heating up and she knew she'd be more careful next Sunday and not hike up her garment on the way up the church steps.

Abigail grabbed her knitted scarf, gloves and hat and rushed down the stairs. As she headed out the back door, she held it so it wouldn't slam. Her mama wouldn't even know she'd gone.

She ran across the yard and around the corner to the livery. Mr. Price glanced in her direction and nodded, but left her to saddle up her own horse. Abigail headed out of town as fast as Herkimer could carry her, stopping only so she could get off and hoist up her skirt and get back on and get some serious riding and praying accomplished.

"Lord, my papa needs healing. His cold has held on long enough." Abigail shouted the words over the north wind whipping around her face. "And, Father, I'd really like the other favor too. Mollie needs to sing four days from today. If You don't step in here pretty quick, I'll be standing center stage instead of my friend."

Herkimer slowed when she eased up on his reins. Abby would give him a few minutes to rest, but her mind still raced as she wondered why the Lord seemed to sit silent on His throne.

His promise in Proverbs a few days before did little to ease her troubled heart that day. But Abigail had to trust. No matter the Lord's silence or if he Himself came down and announced His intensions in her life.

For some reason this tickled Abby and she chuckled, despite her circumstances at the moment. "Yes, Lord, I have to trust."

Abigail tightened her grip on the reins and dug her heel into Herkimer's backside. He took off. As she rode, another issue gnawed at Abigail. Mr. Noah Presley. Why in heaven's name did he go and stir her up the way he did every time she saw him? Again, she thought of last Sunday. She'd caught him sneaking a peek at her bloomers when she lifted her skirt to keep it from getting the hem wet on the church steps.

The moment she noticed him glancing down at her ankle,

her heart leapt so far into her throat she could only muster a smart aleck response when she reached him at the church's massive wooden doors.

Oh, glory be, she'd accused him of seeing apparitions, but what she really hoped and prayed he didn't see was her sporting a pair of her papa's trousers.

This dilemma, coupled with everything else, made Abigail's head hurt. And as fervently as she prayed, she could almost reach out and touch the Lord's silence. Answers seemed as far away as the setting sun. She turned Herkimer around and headed back toward Central City to try to make sense of all the things floating inside her head.

The sunset over the high snowy peaks of the Rocky Mountains announced the late afternoon in brilliant colors. Reds and golds merged in breathtaking fashion, a lovely distraction. Their beauty mesmerized Abby and for a moment she forgot all her troubles. She forgot the bone chilling north wind as it tore at her woolen hat and scarf. Abigail also forgot she hadn't stopped to rearrange herself on Herkimer's saddle. She realized her error when her beloved horse came to a sudden stop on the outskirts of the tiny mining town.

Noah locked up the mercantile as the last rays of sunlight blanketed the western sky. Another long day over and Emma's beef stew beckoned him to hurry across Main Street to Teller House.

Jake Taylor, Noah noticed, stood near the dining establishment. Same as the other day. This time, the banker tarried at the side of the double glass doors, not appearing in a hurry to go inside.

The older man's attention appeared entirely someplace else. He looked up Gilpin Road while he pulled his suit coat closer around himself, buttoning it clear up to his squatty neck. Noah couldn't figure out why the man didn't go in and get in out of the late October cold front.

While Noah questioned his own reasoning for why he ventured out in the cold, he caught sight of Abigail and Herkimer rounding the corner into town. Even from a distance she seemed a bit out of sorts and in a big hurry. Noah would worry about her later—he had other business to attend to at this very moment.

Noah strolled the short distance to the restaurant, fighting against the biting north wind. Its icy fingers grabbed at the skin he'd left exposed. Instinctively, he stuck his ungloved hands in his coat pockets.

"Good evening, Jake. Want to join me for supper, maybe a pie and coffee?" Noah opened the door and stepped back to let the man inside.

"No, son, I'm. . .headin'…"

While Noah waited for the banker to finish his sentence, he let go of the outer door. Figured they'd chat for a minute or two, but Jake didn't continue his conversation. Noah decided to coax him along. Maybe in the end he'd convince the older man to come in and sit down. He still had some questions only he could answer about his pop and the opera house.

"Hey, Jake, if you're turning down a piece of pie, you must be heading somewhere pretty important. Oh, you must be goin' to church?" Noah stated, and then realized it was Thursday evening, not Wednesday. And he remembered he hadn't seen the banker the night before.

"Yes. . .that's right. I'm heading up. . .to church. Getting ready for Homecoming. No. The elder's meet—"

"Is that a fact?"

"Ah huh," the banker answered, but still didn't move a muscle to head up the hill. And from the looks of the snow accumulating on the shoulders of his overcoat, the sparrows would soon start perching on his nearly frozen frame.

Noah chuckled to himself, but knew the banker lied through his teeth. And, his stammering and hem hawing proved it. Along with the fact that he, Mollie and a few others from the congregation practiced at the church the night before.

Both Jake Taylor and Abigail Thompson had been noticeably absent. Mollie Blair explained Abigail's absence. "Her papa's still ailing. I'm certain she'll be here singing on Sunday for the special service."

But Noah didn't hear anyone saying why the banker didn't show.

"Son, I best be headin' that direction. It's getting' late." The fellow sputtered out a few more words before he took a side step to get around Noah.

"It's too bad you're missing out on some of Emma's delicious apple or cherry pie." Noah opened the door once again.

"Mr. Presley, you go on in. No need to worry about me."

He watched Jake as he ambled away in the direction of the church. At the last minute, Noah decided to follow him. Curiosity weighed heavier than his logic at the moment. He stayed a fair distance back and slipped into doorways when Jake would stop and look back over his shoulder. Where his new-found guts came from, he didn't know, but the adventure warmed up his nearly frozen fingers and toes.

Noah watched as Jake Taylor waltzed right past The First Baptist Church on Main Street. This move didn't surprise him. What did was when the older man crossed the street and headed straight to the side of the opera house. Jake looked around before he opened the door and slipped behind it.

"Old man, what are you up—" Noah stopped whispering when he heard the sound of horse's hooves coming down the cobblestone street. He pushed himself farther back into the alcove, but could still see. The man got off and tied his horse to the post at the back of the building. Noah didn't recognize him. Like Jake, he opened the door and went inside.

Noah's heart pounded, but this time the excitement coursing through his veins had to do with something other than Miss Abigail Thompson. His question right then was why in heaven's name would two grown men need to be at the opera house at such a late hour.

And, what in the world he was doing sneaking around after them? There was one thing Noah did know—if someone saw him lurking outside the abandoned building, they'd be calling the sheriff and having him thrown in jail.

He crossed the street and took a couple of deep breaths to calm down before he slowly opened the side door. Noah did his best to make as little noise as possible. He didn't want either of them to hear him.

Loud, but muffled voices came up to greet his nearly frost bitten ears. Noah stopped to listen but couldn't make out a single word the men said.

When the door closed behind him total darkness enveloped him. If he'd have put his hand in front of his face, he wouldn't have seen it. So, before Noah moved an inch, he decided to wait a minute to try to get his eyes to adjust. In no time they did and he could see a sliver of light coming from under a door across the room.

Noah couldn't imagine what his pop stored in the opera house, so to keep from tripping over anything on his trek across the stage, he reached forward with his right hand, and then he tapped his foot lightly in front of him, hoping he'd find his way in the darkness.

The slow process worked like a charm until one swipe of his boot kicked up against something and it got snagged. Noah caught himself and stepped back so he could investigate, but then his other foot slipped out from under him. In that instant, all he could do was fall and do his best not to make a sound, which he didn't accomplish.

His backside landed on the stage with a thud and his elbows made a cracking sound when they hit the wood floor at the same time. The noise echoed clear up to the rafters of the empty building.

Noah lay there for at least a minute, not breathing—in part because he couldn't. The fall knocked the wind out of him. And, the other reason? He thought someone might hear him gasping for air. Sitting up, Noah finally took a deep breath and assessed his damaged areas. Nothing broken, just bruised and a little scraped.

As he got up he found the cause of his spill, the old velvet curtain. The buckle on the side of his boot caught in it. He untangled himself and started out again. This time Noah walked around the yards of material instead of trying to go through it. He inched his way in the direction of the voices, which were now yelling at each other.

"It's simple, Mr. Taylor."

"Mr. Tappen, I'm afraid you don't know who or what you're dealing with. JAR Corp. is huge. Nothing is as simple as you say it is," the banker countered.

"Well, if you think I'm going to stand around this drafty opera house and listen to you, you've got another thing coming."

Noah listened to more loud exchanges going on behind the closed door. His heart went from the pit of his stomach to his throat while he stood there. He trembled as he tried to figure out who or what the two were talking about. In the back of his mind he knew it had to do with the entries in his pop's ledger. He had questions about the same thing.

But, before Noah could have questioned anything, the door he stood in front of flung wide open. It hit the toes of his boots with so much force it slammed back shut, making a resounding bang when it landed. He waited, afraid if he took a breath, it might be his last.

His hiding place had just been found out. *Lord Almighty, have mercy on my soul.*

Eight

"Little lady, I'll take care of Herkimer. You go on home. You don't look too well." Mr. Price took the reins from Abigail's shaking hands.

"No thank you, sir. He's getting special treatment tonight." She smiled at the strange look on the livery owner's face.

Yes, Herkimer would get an extra measure of loving kindness 'cause he saved her from sure embarrassment today. Abigail would be forever grateful to her four-legged friend. If her horse hadn't stopped in time, she'd have ridden into town with her papa's trousers exposed, and maybe even a few other unwomanly attributes to boot.

And to top it off, when she readjusted herself on the side-saddle and rode into Central City like a proper woman should do, she saw Noah Presley. He stood at the mercantile ready to cross Main Street.

Vapors almost overcame Abigail when she thought of how mortified he'd have been if he had seen her riding like some ordinary man. But, with some of the glances he'd been giving her, she felt certain he was smitten with her.

She didn't have time to worry if he was or wasn't interested. Herkimer had saved her from bringing disgrace to her family, maybe even to the tiny mining town. *Thank You, Lord.*

Abigail nuzzled her horse's neck as she brushed his matted coat. The sweat droplets made it glisten in the lantern light. She took off his bridle and hung it on one of the many hooks Mr. Price offered at the livery. "Herkimer, you're a good boy. Do you know you saved me from sure death today? I owe you one."

She patted him as she led him to his stall. Dancer, her papa's horse, stood regal in the next one. Seeing the massive animal brought tears to her eyes. Would her father ever get to ride his horse again? She wondered as she gave him a loving pat on his massive neck. "Oh Lord, you need to heal Papa. Please."

"Miss Thompson. Is that you, Abigail?" Doc Stanton stood breathless on the other side of the livery wall.

"What? Doc Stanton?"

"Come on, I'll explain on the way." The urgency in his voice made her drop the grooming brush.

"It's Papa, isn't it?"

"Go on now, Miss Abigail. I'll take care of him." Mr. Price motioned her toward the door.

Abby ran to the doctor and together they headed up Main Street. With each step her heart beat faster and she could only imagine what awaited them at home.

"Your mama asked me to find you," he explained. His pace hurried with each of his words. Abigail had to pick up her skirt to keep up with him. "Dear, your papa is…" He stopped speaking when they reached the front porch.

"Papa. . .he isn't go—"

"Abigail, you must hurry." Her mama shouted out the front door.

She rushed past her and up the stairs, taking two at a time. Not a stitch of ladylikeness at the moment, but she didn't care. Her papa needed her. Their eyes met as she bound into her parent's bedroom. He gave her a weak smile.

"Oh Papa." Abigail ran to his bed where he lay propped up with pillows. Tears streamed down her cheeks as she plopped down on her knees next to him.

"Please don't cry, daughter." Her papa whispered as he wiped at his own eyes.

She nodded, but couldn't promise him she wouldn't cry. Watching her papa lying there broke her heart into tiny little pieces. Abigail wanted to say so much to him, tell him she loved him with all her heart. That he'd be fine and out riding Dancer in a few days, but the enormous lump in her throat kept her from uttering a single word. She wanted to wake up from this terrible dream.

"Otto, here, take a drink of this."

Her mama's words startled Abigail. She watched her papa struggle to take a sip of water. The simple task caused him to start coughing. He pushed the multi-colored quilt off from across his chest and tried to sit up. When his cough settled down, Mama reached over and wiped the sweat from his brow with her lace handkerchief.

"Abigail, I think it's time you went down to the parlor."

Doc Stanton's words surprised her. *Who does he think he's talking to? I'm not a child. I'm nineteen years old.* She couldn't figure out why she needed to go anywhere, but the tone in his voice told her he meant what he'd said.

"And, Ivy I'd like you to stay." He got into his black bag and brought out a bottle of something. "But, first I'm going to give Otto this so he can get some sleep."

Her mama nodded her head as she walked over to Abigail. Sadness covered every inch of her mama's face. Abigail reached up and grabbed her trembling hand and held on tight. She didn't want to leave her parents. Something might happen. *Lord, where are You?*

"Go on now." Doc Stanton came over and helped her to her feet. Her mama let go of her hand as she backed away. Abigail looked up at the doctor. Deep lines of worry etched themselves around his weary eyes. His grave expression gave her little hope to hold on to. She turned away and walked out to the hallway. Fresh tears erupted and at that moment. Abigail wasn't sure they'd ever stop.

"Ivy, I've tried all I know to try. Otto is in God's hands now."

No, no, no...

Abigail slumped to the chair outside her parent's room. Doc's blunt statement pierced her broken heart. She heard her mama's weeping and wanted to go back to soothe her, but her own pain kept her from moving from the spot she sat.

In the background Abigail heard the downstairs hall clock chime nine bells. She wanted to will its hands to turn back—just two months. Then she could take back all the begging she'd done to get her papa to go on the ride when it ended up raining buckets on them. *Please Lord, I beg You, don't take my papa home.*

"Dear, come now. It's time to go to bed." Her mama's voice surprised Abigail and she realized she must have dozed off waiting for news about her father.

"How is he, Mama?" Abby straightened in the chair,

bracing herself for more bad news.

"I tried to give him some medicine, but he didn't want it," Doc Stanton answered from behind her. "Even without it, he should get some sleep, which he needs and so do both of you."

"We will do just that."

Her mama followed the doctor down the stairs to let him out. She heard her thank him for his trouble, and then Abigail headed to her room to try to get some sleep, but certain it would evade her for another night. Anxiety, mixed with unanswered prayers, and countless other things going on in her head made slumber impossible.

"Lord, I've prayed until I can't pray anymore," Abigail kept her voice down, but she wanted to scream at the top of her lungs. Nothing close to sleep overtook her, even if every fiber inside of her yearned for it. "If I can't sleep, I'll just get up and go downstairs."

She slipped on her flannel robe and her warm booties. On her way out of her room, she stole the heavy quilt off her bed to keep her warm. The embers had died out in her own fireplace, so she guessed the same for the one in the parlor where she headed.

As Abigail quietly made her way down the hall, she thought she heard voices. Her mama's carried so well she could make out some of what she said, but Papa's she decided she'd have to eavesdrop to make his out. Since she'd grabbed her blanket, she decided she'd cuddle up in the hallway and do just that.

Her papa's hoarse voice greeted her as she settled in. "Ivy, I'm sorry I brought you to this *awful* place."

Abigail heard him chuckle and she smiled. She knew her mama hated Colorado and let everyone know it, too.

"And now it doesn't look like Cyrus Presley is going to fix up the opera house," her papa whispered.

"Don't you worry, Otto Thompson. Right now, you're my only concern."

Amen, Mama.

Tears sprang up in Abigail's eyes when she heard her mother begin to cry. Her sobs sounded so much louder in the silence of the late hour. As with her, she knew the emotions of the last few months finally bubbled to the surface and couldn't help but overflow.

Every tear she shed broke Abigail's heart and told of her mama's anguish. And, unless the Lord intervened, their story wouldn't have a happy ending.

"Otto, I too am so sorry I spent all the time fighting with you about us leaving Dallas," her mama's voice carried through the quiet home with a softness Abigail had never heard before.

"My dearest Ivy, you've given up so much for me." Papa coughed so he couldn't go on.

"I didn't give up anything. I wanted to marry you more than sing at the conservatory. Never a regret."

Abigail hoped she didn't gasp when she heard her parents' exchange. *So, this is why Mama always pushes me so hard.*

"If you must know, Mr. Thompson, I married you because I loved you more than anything else on this earth."

"Ivy, you've made a dying man very happy."

Abigail almost jumped up from her hiding place. *Dying man. No!* She couldn't imagine her life without her papa. And she didn't want to think of the possibility of anything as terrible as that happening to them.

"Dear, there's no need to talk about such things, but it is time for you to go to sleep."

Abby didn't hear the rest of the conversation. She dashed back to her bedroom to avoid the chance of getting caught. Her mama didn't shine to people nosing around her business, even if it was her own daughter.

The clock chimed three times and Abigail still stared at the plaster ceiling. She'd heard twelve dings at midnight. Then one and two more an hour later. Still sleep eluded her. Again she got up since she couldn't sleep. This time she stayed in her room, pacing around like a caged animal in the traveling circus.

Her mind couldn't accept her papa dying. In her naïveté, this wasn't how she envisioned her life to turn out. And, if the unthinkable happened, would she also have to leave her beloved Rocky Moun…?

With the unfinished thought bouncing around in her head, Abigail knew she had to escape the confines of her darkened room. She needed to go see her papa, even if she only got to watch him sleep for a minute or two. Her mama bedded down in one of the guest rooms across the hall, so she felt secure she'd be able to peek in on him.

Her feet padded along the wood floor. Every few feet, she'd stop when a squeaky board announced her travel plans. If she stayed still for a moment, the silence would once again wrap itself around her and her journey could continue.

Abigail reached her destination. She poked her head inside and much to her surprise, her papa sat up in bed. This she found strange, noting his condition. Even his coloring seemed much improved from the deathly pallor of earlier evening.

"Papa, what are you doing sitting up? You should be resting." Abigail whispered her statements as she made her way to his bedside.

"I could say the same to you, daughter. Well past your bedtime hour," His voice sounded hoarse from all the coughing. "Come here, you and I need to talk."

"Please don't tell me you're going to die. I don't want to hear it. No." She covered her ears, ready in case he did.

"Abby, Doc Stanton has done all he can, I'm afraid. But, that's not what I want to talk about. Go to Mama's cedar chest and get out the velvet b-box." Her papa stopped to catch his breath. "I-It's right on top."

She got up and did her papa's bidding. When she came back and handed it to him, he told her to open the lid. The minute she did, Abigail saw the small silver locket. The exquisite etching took her breath away.

"I know your birthday isn't for four months, but now is the perfect time to give you my gift."

Abigail took it out of the box and opened the locket and read the words, "I can do all things through Christ which strengtheneth me."

"Daughter, you too can do all things. Trust Him with your singing. With everything in your life. Remember He's given you a gift, use it." Her papa's voice faltered for a moment, and then he added. "I…I love you, my child."

"Oh Papa, thank you."

Abigail smiled and after she clasped the locket around her neck, she reached over to hug her papa. But he started to cough. She poured him a glass of water and tried to give him a drink, but it didn't help. "I'll go get Mama," she spoke through tears of frustration.

Her mother came running down the hall before Abigail could beckon her. She immediately took charge of the dire situation, helping him to swallow some of the honey and lemon mixture left on his side table. Her papa's cough settled right down. A few minutes later his even breathing told them he'd finally fallen asleep.

"Thank you, Mama."

"Abigail Jane, why aren't you, too, in bed?"

"I couldn't s-sleep." Sobs overtook her and she fought to catch her breath. "I had to come see Papa."

Her mama opened her arms and Abigail fell into her welcoming embrace. Their sorrows, together, spilled forth as a rushing river with no dam to stop the deluge. Through her tears, Ivy spoke, softer this time. "Never forget how much your papa loves you."

"Oh Mama, I promise I won't."

The downstairs clock chimed seven times. Abigail and her mama's many prayers had blanketed heaven throughout the late night and into the brand new day. Some of their requests spoken aloud, while others whispered right along with their quiet tears. But, Papa's condition didn't improve. If anything, his breathing became more labored.

Finally, as the clock struck eight, Abigail's father breathed his last and crossed heaven's shore. In a single moment a radiant smile and peace shone bright as the early morning sun across his face. Abby knew her papa sat at the feet of his Lord and Savior. He was back home in the arms of Jesus.

Mama's sobbing broke through the silence of the now quiet bed chamber. Abigail touched her mother's hand, her own tears washing down her face. She was certain they'd never stop and wasn't sure she wanted them to. Her heart lay completely broken inside her chest.

Abigail reached up to touch the precious locket her papa gave her. Fresh tears erupted from deep within her soul for what she'd just lost. *Lord, why didn't You answer our prayers? I can't imagine my life without Papa. Oh, Father, comfort Mama and me. Please help us in the coming days. We're going to need all You've got to give.*

Nine

Noah's nerves still sat on edge after his encounter from the night before. He'd somehow gotten away unnoticed, but before the day ended, he be talking to his father to find out if he knew about the late night rendezvous the banker and Mr. Tappen made to the opera house.

He flipped the *Open* sign over at Presley Mercantile and turned toward the counter. "Maybe, while I'm chatting with Pop, I'll bring up the subject of buying the place."

Since last nights near death experience, the hymn from last Sunday kept rustling through his brain. But for the life of him he couldn't remember a couple of the words. He decided to hum it out loud. Noah almost had it when the mercantile door flew open.

Mrs. Collins stood in the doorway, her eyes wide. "Mr. Presley, have you heard?" She paused and fanned herself with the back of her hand. "Oh, I'm sure you haven't heard. Mr. Otto Thompson went to be with the Lord early this fine morning."

"No, Ma'am, you've made a mistake." Noah picked up his coffee, but put it right back down. His hand shook too much. "Mr. Thompson was just in here the other day."

Mrs. Collins didn't say anything, only placed a tissue to her swollen, red eyes. "Noah, I'm going to take the Thompson's a basket. See if there's anything I can do. I'm sure now they'll head back to Dallas. No need to stay out here in the wilderness and Abigail, she'll need…"

Noah heard the woman babbling on and on, not really listening until he heard Dallas mentioned. His heart twisted inside his chest. *They can't move back to Texas.*

The thought of Abigail leaving made his heart hurt. The pain compounded with the loss of his new friend. Noah took a liking to Otto Thompson and hoped to have many more conversations with him.

The mercantile door swung open again and Noah's father sauntered in. "By the look on your face you've already heard about Mr. Thompson."

"Yes, Mrs. Collins just told me." Noah's voice caught in his throat. He swallowed the lump before he could go on. "Pop, could you watch the place for a while? I'd like to go over and see if there's something I can do for the Thompson's."

"Sorry, son, I can't. I have a meeting with Matthew Tappen." His father backed up toward the door, then glanced his way, concern in his eyes. "Noah, are you alright?"

"Yes, come over here and sit down." Mrs. Collins moved one of the stools over for him and added, "you look like you're goin' to faint."

Noah sat down hard. Indecision racked his insides. He knew he needed to tell his pop about the meeting he'd witnessed at the opera house, but he couldn't blurt it out with

Mrs. Collins there. The town gossip would forget Mr. Thompson's death and have a run away with the latest news.

"Son, are you okay?" His father asked again as he took a couple of steps in his direction.

"Guess the news about Mr. Thompson shocked me more than I imagined." Noah tried to sound convincing, but knew he didn't do a very good job.

"Son, why don't ya just shut the mercantile down? Looks kind of slow at the moment. Go on ahead."

"No, I better stay here. Don't worry about it, Pop. I'll stay—not a problem." Noah stood and walked behind the counter and picked up the broom. He wondered how his father knew anything about the busyness of the store. If he stepped inside, his father didn't stay longer than five minutes.

And why he asked him or Adam to do anything around there was beyond him.

"Mrs. Collins, you have a nice day." Pop tipped his hat and bowed in the woman's direction, and then turned and nodded to Noah before he disappeared behind the curtain and headed out the back door.

Noah noticed that the town gossip didn't acknowledge the older man's farewell. No love lost between the two of them. So when she busied herself with the paltry of ribbon near the stacks of fabric, it didn't surprise him.

He put the broom away and picked up the wet rag and went back to cleaning the counters. Abigail and her mother would have to wait until he closed the shop.

"Noah, I'll watch the mercantile." Mrs. Collins stood in front of him, her hands resting on her ample hips.

"What?"

"You heard me, young man." The authoritative tone in Edna Collins voice told Noah not to ask her to repeat herself.

"I can't ask you to idle away your morning waiting on people."

"Don't you be worrying about me. I can take whatever Presley Mercantile tosses my way. Step aside."

Noah did just that because he believed the older woman could handle almost anything thrown at her, but her gossiping. . .that was another thing.

For the next half hour, Noah taught Mrs. Collins the register and where he kept some items he didn't display out in front. Sometimes merchants asked for things in the personal nature and he kept those hidden behind the curtain. Sure as shooting if he didn't show her, someone would ask and he didn't want her blabbing it all over Central City when she couldn't find the darn thing. When Noah finished, he pulled the curtain back in place.

"Mr. Presley, now go on with yourself. I do believe I have it."

Noah didn't doubt Mrs. Edna Mae Collins had complete control of the situation, so he untied his denim apron and put it under the counter on top of the safe. "Oh, and there is one more thing, if you need change don't worry about it. Just write me a note saying what the person owes and I'll collect it from them later."

The older woman gave him a strange look, but left the statement alone as she went back to tidying up. Noah decided he better tell her or she'd snoop around for a cash box. Knowing Edna, she'd find the place he hid his extra cash. Or worse, she'd locate his Pop's ledger.

As Noah reached for the front door he looked up Main Street. There in a line marched five or six of the ladies from the sewing circle. They headed straight for the mercantile. Part of him wanted to praise the Lord for getting him out of cutting fabric for the next two hours. The other side of him asked, "Will the building survive the bee-hive of activity about to transform Presley Mercantile into something only heaven could imagine?"

"Mrs. Collins, the ladies—"

The door swung open, cutting off Noah's last word. Mrs. Williams strode in front of him, the rest of the ladies followed close behind, all chattering over what each other were saying. He turned back toward his new hired help and she smiled and motioned him to go on about his business of visiting the Thompson's.

As Noah walked up the street, he almost changed his mind about calling on the bereaving family. Would he want someone intruding on him and his family during their time of mourning? He could almost feel his heart answer a resounding *yes*. Noah knew he'd want others around to help comfort him, especially those in his church family. The Lord put His people together for times like these.

Abigail drew back the thick curtains in the parlor. Sun streamed in, encircling her in its warmth. Tears welled up in her eyes just thinking about what today held for her and her mama. Streams of visitors would offer their condolences. She'd rather run as far away as she could. Herkimer needed exercise and she craved time alone with God and her mountains.

As she turned from the window, her eyes caught sight of Noah heading up the front walk. His steps seemed tentative. They slowed even more when he looked up and saw her. Abigail smiled out at her friend, hoping it served as an invitation. Though her heart lay broken from losing her papa, it leapt to her throat when she saw the kindness in the expression he returned.

The door knocker sounded and Mrs. Blair headed to the front door to let the visitor in.

"Welcome, Mr. Presley," Mrs. Blair said after opening the door. "Please come in. The Thompson family is greeting guests in the dining room. Mr. Thompson's body is interned in the parlor." She lowered her voice. "If you'd like, go and take as much time as you need."

Abigail came up to Noah and he extended his hand to her. She grasped it, tighter than planned, and they stood together in the foyer. Her mama cleared her throat from across the room, which made Noah drop Abigail's hand as if it had caught fire. His face flushed deep red.

Abigail cringed when her mama headed toward them. She hoped she wouldn't scold Noah for holding her hand a little too long, considering the circumstances.

"Mr. Presley, it is so kind of you to visit. Otto mentioned how much he enjoyed coming to your mercantile." Abby's mother touched the young man's arm. "And we talked for days about the delicious pie you brought to welcome us to Central City."

"Much obliged, ma'am. I'll sure miss Mr. Thompson."

"As will we all." Mama sighed and tears sprang to her eyes.

"I got into some lively chats with your husband and Samuel Collins over at the mercantile." Noah smiled and his dimple peeked out for a moment. Abigail hoped he didn't catch her staring at him.

"Why don't we come in here where it's more comfortable?" Mrs. Blair pointed into the dining room. "I'll get us some hot spiced tea I just brewed."

"Sophia, you're so kind to come over and help." Abby's mother placed her hand on her friend's shoulder.

"Ivy, it's no trouble. That's what church is all about, helping out when need be. You go sit yourself down now."

Mama took a hold of Abigail's hand and led her over to the table, sitting first, and then patting the chair next to her. Abby sat down, knowing not to question her mama today or any other, for that matter.

Noah followed them into the flowered room and Abigail wondered where he'd sit. She hoped he wouldn't pick the head of the table. Her mama's earlier calmness with him might go right out the window if he did. Relief and a tad bit of joy blanketed her when he took a seat across from them.

Mrs. Blair poured the steaming tea into the delicate china cups and served everyone. "If there's nothing else, Ivy, I'm going on into the kitchen. The dough should be about ready to knead."

"You go right ahead. I'm sure Mr. Presley can get the door if anyone else comes to visit."

As if on cue, the knocker sounded.

"Sit, sit. I'll let them in on my way to the kitchen." Mrs. Blair turned and left the room. Soon voices echoed in the foyer on their way to the parlor area.

Abigail and her mama got up to greet Doc Stanton, who gave them a nod.

"Hello, Mrs. Thompson, Abigail, Noah." The doctor shook everyone's hand. "I know I've said this before, but I'm so sorry for your loss. Otto was a good man."

"You did all you could…" Tears stopped Mama from going on.

Abigail watched her mother struggle to find words and it

broke her heart. She wished everyone would leave. Papa's death was so hard on them and nothing anyone said or did would take their pain away. Only the Lord could soothe their weary souls.

"Mrs. Thompson, it may be a bit too soon to talk about this, but winter's setting in. If you want to head back to Dallas, you might need to make arrangements to do so as soon as possible."

Abigail almost fell off the chair she sat on when Doc Stanton brought up the subject of them moving. She also kept her eye on her mama, who hadn't answered the doctor. Abby wondered if she needed to call Mrs. Blair for some smelling salts or another remedy.

"Doc, after we've buried Otto, I'll make my decision." Abigail's mother sat up straighter in her chair. "By then, my father should be here to help. I know I don't want to stay here, but time will tell."

Abigail jumped up and hurried out the front door. A rushed prayer spilled from her lips and she didn't care who heard. "No, Lord, we can't leave. Papa brought us here. We have to stay. This is our home."

The thought of returning to the hustle and bustle of Dallas almost made Abby sick to her stomach. She wanted to stay here, close to the mountains she'd grown to love. But they weren't the only reason she wanted to remain in Central City. And, at that very moment, Noah came out on the front door. He had become the other reason why Abigail didn't want to leave Colorado.

Noah stepped out on the porch and stayed a short distance

from Abigail. She stood near the railing and faced toward the mountains. He knew the words she prayed out loud came from her mother's last statement.

Also, the young woman's stance today reminded him of one she'd exhibited at the mercantile a day or two after the Thompson's arrival. He remembered her exact words. "The minute I stepped off the train and took in the mountain's splendor, I found my new home. One I never plan to leave."

But after Mrs. Thompson's earlier comment, would Abigail have to leave Central City? Could his heart stand it if she left?

In that moment, Noah questioned why he'd followed her outside. He had enough things on his plate to contend with. Why let his heart get mixed up with Abigail Thompson? That was all he needed, with the opera house situation stirring in his mind.

Abigail turned. "I hope when Gramps sees Colorado, he falls in love with it as much as Papa and I did."

Without thinking, Noah moved to the railing and grabbed her hand again and gave it a tender squeeze. "Miss Thompson, I hope he does too."

Ten

The minute Noah Presley spoke the words out loud he knew he'd do everything possible to keep Abigail Thompson and her mother in Central City. He wanted her to stay as much as she did.

Abigail tugged at her hand, which brought his attention back to the present and Noah let go of it, embarrassed at his boldness for a second time in less than an hour.

"Mr. Presley, I need to go in and check on Mama." Abigail turned toward the front door.

"Yes. I need to get back to the mercantile, too." Noah followed her so he could open the door. "And I'm sure Mrs. Collins is probably thinking I've fallen in by now."

Abigail stopped in front of him, causing Noah to bump into her. Again. *Why does it seem I always follow her too close?* He stepped away from her and she turned to face him.

"Why in heaven's name is Mrs. Blabber—, oh my goodness, I mean Mrs. Collins worried about your whereabouts?"

Noah chuckled at Abigail's slip of the tongue, which made her blush. He watched the pink rise in her cheeks and he wanted to reach up and touch her face, but decided instead he'd better take another step back to steady his heart and his breathing.

When he had both under control he spoke. "I hired her this morning, Miss Thompson since I wanted…" Noah scraped his boot on the wooden porch. "I wanted to come here, to see if there was anything I could do for you and your mother."

Abigail's eyes flooded with tears. "Thank you, Mr. Presley. Right now, the help Mama and I need is your prayers. Losing Papa, it broke both our hearts and Mama's not sure what to do."

"Well, if there's anything I can do, let me know." Noah stepped off the porch and turned around to face Abigail. "There is something I can do. How about for the next month I bring you your supplies? You won't have to worry about coming to get them."

"I'll speak on Mama's behalf on this one and say we'd appreciate your kindness."

Abigail's smile, though sad, warmed Noah clear to his toes. He didn't know helping someone could feel so good.

"Just put your list out here near the door knocker and I'll pick it up tomorrow. Then, if you don't mind, you can leave the back door open and I'll put the supplies inside."

"Thank you, Mr. Presley." Abigail curtsied before she opened the front door. "This will ease Mama's mind. I better go in. She's probably fretting about me by now and thinking we…"

Noah couldn't hear the rest of her sentence. The door shut behind the young woman and he'd have to wonder what he missed.

"Oh there you are," Mrs. Collins loud voice echoed off the board walls of the mercantile after Noah returned.

"Been busy while I was gone?" he asked as he tied his apron on.

"Busier than a hornet's nest in spring time, but Mrs. Busybody kept the place humming along-fine and dandy," Samuel Collins piped up from his corner stool.

Edna Collins reprimanded her husband with the cluck of her tongue. "Mr. Collins, you'd do yourself a world of good if you kept quiet."

Noah couldn't help laughing at the couple standing in front of him. They reminded him of two cantankerous kids having a spat, but knew the two had celebrated their fiftieth anniversary a few months before at a nice luncheon after church.

Can't imagine being married to anyone for so many years.

"What you thinking about, son?" Samuel broke into Noah's thoughts. "One minute you're laughing and next you look like something scared the bewillergers out of you."

"Bewillergers?"

"Noah, don't mind him. Samuel's English isn't always the same taught in school. Sometimes I'm still amazed he can run the telegraph office. Those people on the other end must have learned his language. God bless them. I'm still learning." Mrs. Collins wiped down the counter and handed Noah the rag. "I guess since you're back, I'm relieved of my duties."

"Yes, Mrs. Collins—"

"Noah, before you make any hasty decisions, I think you ought to hire my bride," Mr. Collins interrupted him.

"Samuel, I don't need anyone. Anyway, I've got my brother."

"And I see him about once a month. Son, I've been here for about an hour and she's a selling fool. I'm certain some people came in here today and bought items they didn't want. Edna here could sell dirt to a farmer."

Noah glanced around his store for the first time since he returned. Everything did seem more organized. The stacks of fabric lined up in a perfect rainbow of colors. His counters cleaned of their normal clutter and housed objects people tended to forget and have to come back for. *Brilliant!*

"Mrs. Collins, I'm not sure how you did all this in the short time it took me at the Thompson's, but bless you." Noah scratched his chin and tapped his foot on the wooden floor. "Well, I guess the mercantile has a new employee." As he extended his invitation, Noah questioned his logic.

"Thank you and mark my word, you won't regret your decision."

Noah hoped he wouldn't. *Lord, please let her words be true. I don't want Presley Mercantile becoming known as Central City's Gossip Guild.*

Abigail came down early the next morning with a two-fold purpose in mind. First she hoped she'd catch a glimpse of Noah. When he tried to finagle the back door, she'd appear at the right moment to help him. Try not to seem too obvious. Her only problem, the store owner didn't say the exact time he'd bring their supplies.

Now to the second reason she got out of bed. She'd brew some fresh coffee. If she pampered her mama with her favorite beverage, maybe she could slip out later and venture a ride on Herkimer. With Mrs. Blair coming in to help, she could take care of the people still visiting Papa.

"I just have to get out of here and breathe some crisp mountain air. If I don't, I'll go completely nuts."

"Abby, are you talking to yourself again?"

Mollie Blair's voice startled Abigail. She didn't expect her and her mother so soon. Noah's face was the one she truly wanted to see.

Her friend came in, carrying a bag of sugar and a satchel full of beans. Mollie's mother followed a few steps behind with her arms laden down with cornbread and a large roasting pan.

"Here, let me help you, Mrs. Blair." Abigail grabbed a bag from the older woman and set the cornbread on the counter near the sink.

Mollie came over and poked Abigail in her rib. "I know you're trying to ignore my question. You sounded like you were jabbering nonsense when Mother and I came in."

"It probably did. Yes, I was chattering to myself," she admitted. "And, I'll say it again. If I don't get away from this house for a bit—I might lose my common sense, as well."

Mollie laughed. "Girl, with all you've been through with losing your papa, no one could blame you."

"She's right, dear. You go on up and change into your riding gear. I'll take care of your mama. Not to worry." Mrs. Blair shooed Abigail out of the room and went to work tidying up the kitchen. "And, you too, Mollie, you go on up there and help her."

They hurried upstairs, but their normal laughter and gaiety hidden away for today. Didn't want to disrespect her papa. Abigail wanted with all her heart to take in the magnificence of the Rocky Mountains, but taking a ride without her papa seemed almost beyond her comprehension.

Mollie helped Abby out of her dark gray smock, having to yank and pull the folds of fabric to get the task accomplished.

"I don't know why women have to wear all of this stuff." Mollie tossed the garments onto the bed.

Abigail stood in her bedroom donned in only her lace petticoat. "Mollie, can you keep a secret?"

Her friend nodded and let out a high-pitch giggle.

Abigail raced over to her closet and got on her hands and knees, rummaging clear in the back of it for her secret stash. She smiled when she found the item and started backing out. The next thing she knew, part of her hair caught under her knee.

"Ouch. That hurt. Mollie, I swear, one of these days I'm going to whack all this mess off." Abigail pulled her blond hair out of her face and stood up.

"Girl, what in heaven's name do you have in your hand?"

"That's my secret. I wear 'em when I ride Herkimer. I 'borrowed' a pair of Papa's trousers and tried them out. Oh my gracious, Mollie. Freedom! And what a kick in the pants to ride just like the men do." Abigail laughed at her unintended pun and the expression worn on her friend's face at the moment.

"That's. . .that's absolutely disgraceful."

Abby waggled her index finger in her friend's direction. "Don't judge or lest ye be judged."

"Quoting Bible verses isn't going to keep the wrath of the Almighty from striking you down for wearing men's clothing."

"But no one knows I have them on, Mollie. I put on my riding outfit and the long skirt covers what's hiding underneath."

"What happens when you walk?"

Abby could see the excitement brewing in her friend's eyes. "Let me show you." She put on the pants and cinched them at the waist. Next, Abigail slipped her riding dress over her head. The yards of material tumbled down over her small frame, covering all evidence below.

To further convince her friend, she strolled across her bedroom. All stayed covered. No one would ever suspect.

"Incredible."

"Told you. So, now can I count on you to keep my secret?"

Mollie leaned against the door and started tapping her index finger on her chin. "Well, I don't know. I could use this knowledge to my advantage. Let me think about this."

They chuckled as they headed downstairs. Abigail shushed them as they neared the kitchen and she hoped she could slip out before her mama caught wind of what Abby planned to do, but no such luck.

"Abigail Thompson, get in here," her mother's voice resounded from the dining room.

She walked into the room and her mama sat at the far end of the mahogany table near the bay window. "Yes, Mama."

"Daughter, Mrs. Blair informed me of your plans." Abigail's mother paused and took a drink of her coffee.

Abby's heart sank, knowing what would come next.

"And I honestly think it's an excellent idea. Your papa would want you to go out and enjoy God's creation. I know he's up in heaven right now smiling down on us."

Abigail went over to her mama and gave her a hug. "Thanks. I promise I won't be too long."

Eleven

"Mr. Presley, it's high time you showed back up."

"I'll be right there Mrs. Collins," Noah answered her after he'd barely gotten the back door propped open. *She's starting on me again. Why, oh why did I hire this woman...*

Noah didn't get to finish the not-so-complimentary assessment of his new employee because his foot slipped off the top step. The railing saved him from falling to the hard ground, but in the process his boot kicked the door and it slammed shut on the extra supplies he'd brought back from the Thompsons.

"So much for Mrs. Collin's homemade bread."

"Mr. Presley, I don't know what you're doing out here, but finish it up. I need your help in here." Mrs. Collins reached down and picked up the crumpled bag and headed back inside. "Well, are you coming, son?"

"I'll be right there." Noah headed over to the wagon to grab the flour sack and hoisted it over his shoulder. He went up the stairs without incident this time, but the conversation on the other side of the curtain caught his attention.

To most anyone listening, it sounded like a busy beehive in the springtime. He pulled the partition aside and could feel his chin almost drop to his chest. People stood everywhere in the mercantile, each holding merchandise and jabbering and jawing with other customers.

Lord, I don't know what's going on, but forgive me for any bad thoughts I might of had concerning Edna Collins. She's an angel.

"Looks like you better put that sack down and get to work." Samuel Collins winked at Noah.

"Mr. Presley, you don't have time to talk to my husband—who, by the way, needs to get back to work. Now, did you get me down the case of pickles I asked for?"

Noah didn't remember her asking, but he jumped to it as if he'd been shot. Up and down the ladder he ventured, much to his dismay. On his last trip down, Noah decided she barked out orders better than any General ever did in the United States Army.

So, when Noah finally turned the *Closed* sign over at the end of the day, he couldn't remember ever being so busy or tired. He walked over to the cash register and started to count the money. His till tonight would surely boost his saving's account.

With monies in hand, he'd finally bring up the all-important question to his pop about selling him the opera house. His dream was only a few dollars away from reality.

And, while I'm at it, I'll ask him why his business partner and banker visited the place at such a late hour the other night.

The bell over the door rang out. *Guess I forgot to lock the door.*

"Noah, is Edna still here?" Samuel asked. "I'm hungry."

"No, she left about ten minutes ago. Must have headed up Main instead of Eureka."

"Sometimes that woman." Samuel Collins waved his hand and left before he finished his sentence.

"Yes, sometimes that woman amazes me and infuriates me all at the same time. But, whatever she is doing here at Presley Mercantile, I hope she keeps doing it."

Noah shut the lights out and headed upstairs. Tomorrow the mercantile would close and the little town of Central City, Colorado would mourn the loss of Mr. Otto Thompson. A sad day, but one the Lord would surely be honored and glorified in.

"Mama, can I come in?" Abigail knocked on her parent's bedroom door. She waited, but no answer came. Abby headed back to her room. With each step her dark gray skirt made a rustling sound in the quiet stillness of the morning. The cold wood floor beneath her bare feet reminded her she'd forgotten her stockings. She hurried down the long hallway, jumping from one foot to the other.

"Abigail, please hurry. Reverend Blair should arrive any minute, so quit fooling around and get down here."

How does she always know what I'm doing? Even in Mama's grieving she could reprimand with the best of them. Abby rushed to put on her black boots and tied them up. Didn't want to tarry a moment longer. The Reverend or Mama wouldn't have to wait on her today.

Abigail made it down the stairs in record time. The second

she graced the doorframe of the kitchen, she heard, “Daughter, Mr. Presley came over extra early this morning to bring the special flowers for the ceremony today.”

Her mama scurried about the kitchen. Before long she left the room and into the parlor, making Abby almost dizzy from her tidying up the already spotless room. If Abigail hadn’t seen this behavior before at her grandmother’s funeral, she’d think her mama was getting ready for a social engagement instead of an internment.

She remembered asking her mama why she didn’t cry at Granny’s service.

“Abigail Jane, people don’t want to see other’s tears. They want to see everyone and everything under control. So, I make sure I’m poised for everyone to see. Always the hostess. Tears can come later, Abigail, when you’re alone to grieve.”

“Mama, I’m sure no one expects you to hold it together.”

The sound of the knocker interrupted Abigail’s recollection and she went to answer the door. Reverend and Mrs. Blair stood outside.

“Please come in. Mama’s already in the parlor.” Abigail showed them into the room. “Please sit anywhere you want.”

The Reverend gave her a little nod. “Thank you, dear.”

Abigail walked past Papa’s casket on her way out. The sight of him broke her heart. She knew if she tried to display nerves of steel like Mama, she’d lose the battle at hand. The tears of sadness and so much more would tumble from her eyes and no one would tell her to do otherwise.

As the last guest left, Abigail felt dazed. The afternoon blurred in her mind and she couldn’t even remember what Reverend

Blair said about her papa. She didn't worry, though. Someday she'd ask someone, maybe Noah or Mollie, to tell her about the words the pastor spoke.

Lord, thank You for giving me my papa. Even for such a short time. I still don't know what I'm going to do without him, but You're in control. Be with Mama tonight and help her grieve in the only way she knows best. Lord, You are our comfort and our strength. In Jesus' name. Amen.

Twelve

The back door of the mercantile squeaked when Noah opened it after Mr. Thompson's service and the dinner afterwards. The late afternoon light cast a shadow across the floor of the mercantile. He blinked at the sun's brightness reflected on the far window pane and a tear slipped down from the corner of Noah's eye. His heart ached for Abigail.

He decided he'd work on his books then he'd go up to bed. Put the sad day to rest. Close to three hours later, and happy with his checks and balances working out, Noah changed into his pajamas.

The melody of *Amazing Grace* that he heard played at Mr. Thompson's funeral kept him company while he changed. Hearing the sacred song always brought out mixed emotions for Noah.

The song reminded him of his beloved grandmother and it made him smile. Without Gram he wouldn't possess his love for music or the desire he had to restore the opera house to what it once was when she owned it.

"Dear, you have such an ear for music," she told him the day he played *Amazing Grace* for the first time, so many years before.

Noah had looked up from the keys. He didn't have a clue what his grandmother was talking about. "Ear for music? Can I hear better 'cause of my big ears?

Gram laughed. "Heaven's no. Noah, God's given you a special gift. You hear a song and can play it without a stitch of music sitting in front of you."

Noah shrugged his shoulders and plunked out *I'll Fly Away* without batting an eye. His grandmother clapped her hands and tapped her foot to the rousing rendition of the old hymn.

"I should have figured I'd find you in here doing that sissy stuff," Pop's booming voice stopped the lively tune mid-tempo.

Noah snatched his hands off the keys and glanced up at his father, almost afraid the big man would pluck him right off the bench.

"Cyrus, your son is practicing his God-given talent and we've only got another five minutes to go. I think whatever you need can wait that long." Gram emphasized every word she spoke.

Noah's father stood a foot taller than his mother, but instead of standing his ground, he took a couple of steps back before speaking again. "He needs to be outside helping me, so make it fast."

With that, Pop turned and stomped out of the parlor. Gram gave him a compassionate look. "Dear one, don't listen to your father. He doesn't know what he's talking about. You're not a sissy. That's for sure."

His grandmother's words from years before resonated in

Noah's mind as he turned off his lamp. "Gram, I might not be a sissy, but I am afraid to ask Pop for what's rightfully mine. One things for sure, scared or not, I will find a way to own the opera house. Even if I have to spend the last dime I have to get it done."

Noah turned over on his lumpy mattress and punched at his down pillow before settling his head into it. He shut his eyes, but his jumbled thoughts kept him awake. Sleep finally overtook him at dawn.

The rooster crowed outside Noah's window way too early and he slid his aching body out of bed. His eyes, when he finally got them to open, felt like he needed to prop them open with something. *I can tell it's going to be a long day.*

"Mr. Presley, are you up there?"

Noah heard Mrs. Collins' chattering downstairs, and the long day ahead of him just developed a voice. "Yes, I'm here. I'll be down in a few minutes." He berated himself for giving the older woman a key, but decided he didn't have time right then to worry himself about it. He needed to get dressed 'cause his customers wouldn't appreciate his flannel bed-clothes.

He dressed and then entered the store with a bright greeting. "Good morning, Mrs. Collins. How are you this fine morning?" Noah didn't feel anywhere close to the perkiness he exhibited, but a sour disposition would get him in trouble.

"Pray tell, young man, what in the world is wrong with you?" Mrs. Collins tidied up the counter, giving Noah a worried glance over her spectacles.

"Just greeting the day, that's all. Remember, this *is* the day which the Lord hath made; we will rejoice and be glad in it." *I'm slathering the butter on thick now.*

"Guess I should call it my lucky day when I can get a smile and a verse out of you before your first cup of coffee."

She moseyed on over to the pot and poured Noah a cup.

"Edna, you might want to do that one more time, since you forgot to make me any this morning," Samuel Collins announced this as he walked into the mercantile and perched himself on his normal stool in the corner.

Noah glanced up at his friend and noticed him winking at his wife who stood behind the counter. She swatted him with the rag she had in her hand, and then she must have realized what she'd done and she grinned. A pinkish blush touched her chubby cheeks.

"Ya old coot, I left your coffee simmering on the stove, along with your oatmeal. Don't tell me you didn't see it sitting there?"

"Yes, I saw those dried up oats. Before I left, I fed them to the cat." Samuel looked at Noah and their laughter filled the mercantile.

Noah could tell Mrs. Collins didn't see the humor in her husband's admission of feeding his oats to the stray tabby, but before she could add her two cents, her husband chimed in. "Edna, you know I have to give you a heap of trouble since Mr. Presley and his store's getting all your attention."

Noah nearly choked on the sip of coffee he took when he heard his friend's last statement, but quickly recovered. "I believe you're the one who suggested your wife for employment at this fine establishment." Noah walked over to the coffee pot and poured himself another cup. "Need a warm up, Samuel?"

"No, I'm fine. I better be heading over to the telegraph office before I get into too much more trouble with Edna Mae." The old man cackled.

"Mr. Collins, I think that's a grand idea." Mrs. Collins walked her husband toward the front door. "And, Mr. Presley, you better be getting yourself over to the Thompson's. They are probably looking for their supplies."

Noah glanced at the wall clock and realized he needed to get some work done and quit bantering with Mr. and Mrs. Collins. He scooted out the back door and loaded up the wagon; his tiredness a mere memory now, thanks to the two cups of coffee he consumed.

"Mrs. Collins, I won't be long," Noah opened the door and shouted inside, hoping the woman heard.

"Don't worry about me, Mr. Presley, take your sweet time."

Noah smiled at Mrs. Collins's comment as he boarded the wagon and headed out. He knew the town gossip relished getting to spend any part of her day in the busy mercantile without him around. This gave her plenty of time to collect all the fodder she needed for weaving tales about the town folk.

"Lord, all I ask is that you give her enough sense to not babble everything she hears. Give her discernment." The minute the last word fell out of Noah's mouth he thought of his father. "And, Lord, while You're at it, Pop could also use an extra measure of it. Maybe then he'd quit falling up to his eyeballs in every new scheme that comes up the pike."

Noah reached Abigail's home and the thoughts of Mrs. Collins and his father drifted out of his mind. He hummed his favorite hymn as he started to unload the items off Mrs. Thompson's list.

Abigail heard the wagon and rushed to the window to see Noah. She watched from the kitchen as he brought their goods to the back door. Before her brain kicked in to stop her, Abby dashed out to the porch and stood next to the pantry. Right in the store owner's way.

"Good morning Miss Thompson."

Noah tried to step around Abigail, but when he zigged—she zagged. This maneuver with each other went on for a second or two before Abby stopped moving and said, "Sorry, didn't mean to get in your way." She gestured him forward and felt her cheeks growing warmer as he passed by.

"Not a problem. Always love to try and miss stepping on the toes of such a pretty young woman at eight-thirty in the morning."

Abigail smiled at him, unable to utter a sound. She wondered if she pinched herself that she'd wake up and it would only be a dream. *Did Noah just say what I thought he said? Oh my goodness.*

"Mr. Presley, it would do you well to finish up your delivery. I'm also sure Abigail doesn't need to help you." Abby's mother appeared in the doorway, staring at both of them.

"I'm sorry, Mrs. Thompson. I. . .we. . .I'll finish and get out of here."

Abby watched Noah's coloring go from pink to crimson in the matter of a few seconds. The smile and his sweet dimple faded as he collected his belongings.

"Mr. Presley, please excuse me." Abigail scooted past the store owner. Embarrassment wore heavy on her heart for what her mama said to Noah. She stopped just long enough on the back porch to grab her woolen cloak out of the hall closet before running out the door to Herkimer and a much needed time with her heavenly Father.

Mr. Price must have seen her coming. He had her horse saddled and ready to go. Abigail hoisted herself into the saddle and took off in whatever direction Herkimer decided to go. She didn't care.

"Lord, I thought Mama's heart had started to soften toward Noah, but I guess not."

Abigail reached Digger's Gulch and hopped off Herkimer, tying him to a nearby tree in the meadow. Her face stung from the morning chill.

In her haste to leave, she'd forgotten her hat and scarf. Abby placed her gloved hands on her cheeks, hoping this would help warm them up. Gentle snow began to fall around her and she beheld the beauty of the snowcapped mountains all around her.

So much had happened in such a short time, which she could do nothing about. But Abigail Jane Thompson knew for certain on two things. She'd fallen madly in love with the Rocky Mountains and Mr. Noah Presley. Now she had to figure out a way to stay where Papa planted his family.

Thirteen

Snow swirled around Digger's Gulch. Before it got any deeper Abigail decided she and her horse, Herkimer, better high tail it on home. She didn't want her mother sending out a search party looking for her wayward daughter. Why add fuel to the already burning fire?

Abigail knew she had to tell her mama the truth about her quick departure, but she'd have to figure out a more creative way of getting it accomplished. Blurting it out wouldn't shine too well. She'd have to line it all up and tie it in a pretty little bow by the time she got back to Central City.

"Mama, I don't think Mr. Presley meant any harm saying I'm beautiful." Abigail stopped and almost swooned. "Did I really hear right? Did Noah Presley say I'm beautiful?"

Abigail wanted to believe he said such a nice thing, but she still had a dilemma of what to say to her mama. Thoughts twirled around in her head as she and Herkimer made their slow trek back home.

"Herkimer." Abigail patted her horse's neck. "On second

thought, I better leave Noah out of this. The mention of his name might cause Mama's blood to boil and I don't want that to happen."

As if he answered, Herkimer shook his head from side to side." The sight of her horse's actions made her laugh. She wanted to stop and share the memory with her papa, but she couldn't. The pain of his death sat heavy on her heart. She touched the precious locket he gave her and smiled.

"Papa, I can do all things through Christ who strengthens me. Even if the 'all' sometimes includes Mama and her way of talking to people. Or even if she doesn't like Noah right at the moment. Oh, Papa, I miss you so much and I have to tell Mama the truth. The truth about a whole wagon load of things."

Abigail wiped the lone tear away with her gloved hand and turned down Main Street into the little mining town. Her stomach tied in a knot thinking about her mother. Herkimer slowed as he neared the livery.

Mr. Price stood talking to a young man she didn't recollect seeing around Central City. *But a handsome addition he'll make if he moves here.* Abigail chided herself for her unladylike thought as she jumped off her horse.

"Good morning, miss. You do ride at some of the strangest hours." Mr. Price took Herkimer's reins.

"Oh, not at all, sir. Not at all. Every moment of every day is a good time for a ride. Until the Lord Himself comes and takes me to my heavenly home, you'll find me venturing out in this spectacular scenery. Summer, winter, spring or fall."

"Or when Mama suggests her daughter quit traipsing about town."

Abigail almost jumped out of her not-so-ordinary riding clothes she wore. She stared at her mother and all the rehearsing she'd done on the trail went out of her brain in a puff of smoke. If the stranger asked for her name, Abigail wasn't sure she could remember it at that very moment.

"M-mama?"

"Yes, Mama, and I think it's time you get yourself home. If people see you out here they're goin' to wonder what kind of daughter your papa and I raised."

The young man now smiled at Abigail. His blue eyes were the color of the sky. She felt her cheeks burning as she turned away and blamed it not on the handsome stranger, but on the cold November day.

Mama led the way through the snow-covered streets of Central City. Abigail followed close behind. They both stomped their feet in unison when they reached the front porch of their yellow Victorian home. No other sound came out of either one of them on the walk home.

Abby's normal chatty nature completely clammed up when she'd seen the look on her mother's face at the stable. The quiet continued as they draped their damp cloaks across the pegs on the hall tree.

Her mother broke the silence as they stood in the foyer. "Daughter, I don't know what comes over you sometimes."

"Honestly, Mama, I can't figure me out either." Abby glanced at her mother, hoping she'd catch a hint of a smile. She didn't and decided to add, "I'm pretty sure others in this little town are baffled as you are about Abigail Thompson, too."

That statement brought a grin to her mother's face, even though Mama tried to hide her happy expression with covering her mouth with her hand. It didn't work. Abigail could still see it peeking out.

Abby wanted to chuckle, but decided not to press her luck.

But, oh, how she enjoyed when she found a way to soothe a situation with her sassiness. She knew it didn't happen all the time with Mama, but had always worked like a charm with her papa.

"Daughter, if your shenanigans don't get the best of me; they are going to turn me completely gray. I just don't know." Her mother walked toward the kitchen, her steps echoing in the hallway. "Come on in here, Abigail, let's get us some of the chicken soup Mrs. Blair made for us for dinner. Then we'll sit in front of the fireplace and dine."

"What? We've never eaten anywhere but at the kitchen or dining room table. Never in the parlor." Abigail knew she must have given her mother a strange look.

Her mama laughed this time. "Can't I do something out of the ordinary once in a while? You do it all the time."

"Sure. I guess you can." Abigail wondered if someone came in and took her mama while she ventured out with Herkimer.

Her mother headed over to the stove and filled up two bowls with a ladle of steaming chicken soup. The savory aroma of spices filled the room. Abigail came up and took the dishes and carried them on the tray Mama arrayed with bread, butter and a jar of jam.

"I'm starving."

"Well, daughter, you did miss breakfast when you went out on your escapade today."

"Guess I did. Sorry."

"Let's take this into the parlor and eat. I'm famished myself. Anyway, Abigail, I have something important to tell you."

Again Abby wanted to turn tail and run again. *I know what Mama's going to say. She's going to take us back to*

Texas. Lord, please answer my prayer on this one. I don't want to leave Colorado. Please!

Tonight, Noah decided, would be the time he'd talk to his pop about the meeting at the opera house he'd witnessed back a few weeks before. *No time like the present.* His father would return that evening from another trip to Denver and Noah needed to chat with him before he changed his mind.

He busied himself around the mercantile after coming back from the Thompson's. Funny, the conversation with Mrs. Thompson from the day before hadn't been mentioned and the woman seemed a little more cheerful toward him. *Strange, but thank goodness for small favors.*

Abigail on the other hand didn't appear happy at all and Noah couldn't figure out why. No doubt her mood had something to do with her mother. He hadn't had a chance to speak to her, but planned to talk to her Homecoming Sunday after her much anticipated solo performance.

"Mabel Pederson, what on earth are you wearing on your shoulders?"

Mrs. Collins voice rang out through the mercantile and brought Noah back to the place of business. Every eye, which had been looking at merchandise inside the wooden structure, now jerked their heads around to see about the commotion

"Well, Edna Mae, if you'd read the latest fashion magazines out of New York City you'd know what I am wearing. Obviously with what you have on, you're not privy to the latest styles."

"If wearing a dead skunk around your neckline is fashionable, please don't subscribe me to their catalogs."

"Well I never..." Mabel tossed what looked like a tail over her left shoulder and stomped in the direction of the door. With each of her steps, the head of the animal bobbed up and down on her back.

How Noah kept from laughing at the unprecedented site could only be called a true answer of prayer. He rushed over to the front door to try and keep Mrs. Pederson inside his mercantile, even for a minute so he could explain. "Ladies, ladies, ladies" was all that came out of his mouth. He couldn't think of anything else to say to calm the woman down.

Mrs. Pederson came to a halt in front of him. Their noses a mere two inches from each other. "Mr. Presley, I'd hope you'd hire someone a bit more knowledgeable in the area of fashion, but it's obvious you didn't. As long as *she* works here, I'll not frequent your establishment. Now if you'll excuse me."

Other than tackling the older woman to keep her in his store, Noah had to step aside and allow her to go around him through the opened double doors. Her entourage of other church ladies followed, leaving he and Edna Collins alone in the mercantile.

Noah released a groan then said, "Mrs. Collins, I can't believe you just said those things."

"Now, young man, I wouldn't be lecturing me. That old bat wouldn't know a fur stole from road kill if it came up and chewed her nose off."

Again Noah searched for the right words and none came. Maybe he'd have a talk with Samuel, see if he could give him some advice. God love his friend—but at the moment questioned how he'd made it fifty years with the woman standing in front of him.

Lord, could you tell me again why I hired this woman?

The bell over the door chimed and three of the four

women came back inside the store. Their continuous chattering told Noah that Mrs. Pederson decided lunch at The Teller House sounded better than heading up to church to decorate for Homecoming Sunday.

"Edna, we couldn't wait to tell you this piece of news. Can you believe she isn't going to help decorate? Mabel's getting too big for her britches, I'd say." Mrs. Abbott nodded toward the door.

Noah busied himself with stocking the shelves, but kept one eye on the ladies. He stayed close enough to monitor what Edna Collins might pull next. A few more tidbits flowed within the group of church ladies, but for the most part none could classify as earth shattering. Noah headed to the backroom to get some more stock, but Mrs. Collins's voice stopped him right behind the curtain.

"Oh, I promised Samuel I wouldn't tell anyone about the telegram, but I can't keep this under my bonnet any longer." The group of women gathered around Mrs. Collins. She took out a piece of paper and said, "I jotted this down when Samuel wasn't looking, so bear with me."

"Would you hurry up."

"Shush. I'm trying to read my own writing. I think it says, Mr. Reardon is due to arrive on Monday, November fifth. The day after tomorrow." She glanced up from the paper. "He's Ivy Thompson's father, for those of you who don't know. I'm sure she can't wait to see him after all she's endured. I have it on good authority he's coming to take them back to Dallas."

Noah didn't have a mirror, but he knew his mouth hung wide open with this juicy piece of gossip dumped in his lap.

Fourteen

"Mama, I'm tired of singing and I think I hear Herkimer calling me. He wants me to take him for a ride." Abigail glanced out the parlor window. The sunny November day beckoned her to come out and visit, but her mama kept insisting she practice her solo for the next day at church.

"Your lame attempt at getting out of music lessons will not work with me today." Her mother strummed her fingers on top of the grand piano. "And, anyway dear, do you think me daft that I'd believe a horse sends you messages?"

"No ma'am, the truth is Herkimer doesn't talk to me, but he sure listens when I need him to. Something you'd do…" Abigail threw her hand up to her mouth. Certain this time her sassiness would send her into more than her share of deep trouble.

"Daughter, that's just about enough out of you. When your grandfather arrives on Monday, you'll do well to keep still." Abigail's mother stepped from behind the piano and took a seat in her husband's chair. "Dear, I know why you've had a snippy attitude for the last week or so, but it's not going to change the fact that we are going back to Texas. And that's final."

"See, I told you. You never listen. I'll say it one more time. I'm not leaving Colorado when Gramps comes to get us." Abigail stormed out of the parlor and ran up the stairs to her room.

She slammed her door and the photos on her wall rattled. Abigail didn't care whether they fell off.

"Lord, she's not listening to reason." Abby whispered through the deluge of tears streaming down her face. "We have to stay. Papa brought us here for a reason. He loved us too much to just dump us here in the middle of nowhere. There's another purpose, I'm sure of it."

She couldn't go on, her anger and anguish silenced any more of her words. Abigail's resolve crumpled and she sat down hard on the wood floor and wept. Evening shadows filled the room as the sun set on another day.

Abigail heard a light tap on her bedroom door. "Daughter, please let me come in. Can we talk?"

She ignored the request, not wanting to see her mother or anyone else, for that matter. Even if she let her mama in, she still wouldn't have the answer Abby wanted to hear—that they would stay in Colorado and make Central City their home.

Abigail woke up and her body ached. She stretched her arms above her head and yawned. Memories of the argument with Mama festered in Abby's mind and she could feel her brow furrow as she lay in bed.

She stayed burrowed under the covers since when she did get up she'd have to face her mother. If that wasn't enough, Abigail would have to tend with gawking parishioners when she sang her solo. She assumed they waited for her to take a plunge off the stage. Like last time.

"Lord, how majestic is Your name." Abby hoped starting her prayer with praise would up her standing. Couldn't hurt. A catch in her spirit prompted her to say a heartfelt, "Sorry, Father."

The grandfather clock in the hallway started to chime. Abigail snuggled deeper into her bed and counted "five, six, seven. Seven o'clock." Her feet hit the cold floor and she shivered as she jumped out from under the quilt. "What is going on? Mama should have gotten me up by now. She must really be mad at me."

Abigail lit her hurricane lamp sitting on her night table and headed to her wardrobe. As she passed the fireplace in the corner of the room, she noticed the fire had almost died out from the night before. She shivered as she placed three logs on the embers. Soon the wood ignited. Her room warmed up as she picked out what to wear.

She decided her black wool mourning dress and short jacket would do for the morning's activities at church. Abigail left her papa's trousers hidden away for another day and slipped her skirt over her head.

As she did, her hand brushed the locket Papa gave her. His words echoed in her mind. *"Daughter, you can do all things through Christ who strengthens you."*

Abigail could almost hear her papa's voice in the stillness of her room while she finished getting dressed. Oh how she wished she could wake up and the last three weeks hadn't happened. That he'd be sitting at the table, drinking his mug of coffee when she made it downstairs to the kitchen. Sadness filled her heart.

"Papa, I hear your words, but singing in front of the congregation, I'm not so sure that's one of the things I can do. And, right now I'm praying I don't have to."

Again Abigail's thoughts went to faking an illness and letting Mollie take her place, but she put them aside and finished buttoning the last button on her jacket. She then patted the precious locket with her right hand. *I love you, Papa.*

Abigail headed over to the window and wondered why her mama hadn't woken her up. She opened the thick brocade curtain and the sight she beheld almost took her breath away. Snow drifted two feet higher than the railing around their porch. White mounds glistened in the early morning sunshine.

"Thank You, thank You, thank You, Lord. My prayers have been answered." Abigail put her hand over her mouth. She hoped her exuberance at not having to sing had stayed behind the dark mahogany door. Didn't want to add anything else to annoy her mother.

But, just in case, she opened her door and peeked out; still no sign of Mama. So she hadn't heard Abby's shouts of joy. Abigail turned around and waltzed her way around her room a couple of times.

"Daughter, what on earth are you doing?"

Abigail spun around and faced her mother. "Uh, nothing. Just—"

"Just what. Now you're dancing on Sunday. The Lord is goin'. . .Never mind. Finish getting ready. Remember, it's your big day."

"Mama, come here and look. Haven't you seen it?"

"Seen what?"

Abigail pointed out of her floor to ceiling window.

"Oh my gracious sakes," Her mother said as she strode over to the window in full mourning regalia. Her matching parasol over her right arm.

"This ghastly weather, that's exactly why I don't want to stay here."

Abigail decided at that moment that nothing Mama said today would spoil her festive mood. And the grin splashed across her face told her mother, and the world, how happy the inclement weather made her.

"Abigail, may I ask you something?" her mama glanced outside again. "Why does four feet of nonsense make you smile?"

"Mama, didn't you know I love snow?" Abby couldn't contain her happiness.

"You're fibbing, daughter, and I know it. You complained every time in Dallas when the snow fell. This isn't any different."

Funny how her mother always caught her in her fibs. Might have something to do with her now sheepish expression she knew she wore when the cat came out of the bag. "Yes, Mama, this snow is…"

"Is what? Oh I know, you think this little skiff of snow is going to keep you from singing this morning."

"Mama, you might want to take a closer look." Abigail held the curtain back and as she did she heard her mother gasp then said, "I don't believe we're going anywhere."

"No, Abigail, I don't think we are, but Mr. Presley is."

She rushed up to the window and looked out to see what her mama was talking about. Noah's head appeared above the massive drift that blocked their front door. His arms wielded a spade and he used it to clear the white mountain off their porch.

"Mama, we need to hurry up and fix him some hot cocoa." Abigail announced as she let the curtain fall back into place.

"Not so fast, dear." Abigail's mother touched her arm. "Before you chase after your young man, we need to talk about your behavior last night."

"But Mama, I have to save Noah." Abigail turned to head out of her room, but her mother moved and blocked her way.

"But Mama, nothing. Mr. Presley is going to stay out there until you talk to me and tell me you're sorry for your brashness last night."

Abigail knew if she didn't say something soon, Noah would surely freeze to death, but her stubbornness kept her lips sealed.

"So be it."

Her mother walked past her without another word and started down the long stairway. Abigail followed her into their darkened kitchen where Mama lit the lamps near the sink. Abby loaded the logs in the fireplace.

"While I heat up the milk for the hot cocoa, we'll talk. Remember, daughter, the sooner you apologize, the sooner Mr. Presley gets to warm his chilled extremities."

Abigail lined the kindling in perfect horizontal and vertical lines, stuffing newsprint underneath to get the flames lapping over the mighty logs. *Lord, You answered my prayer about my singing. Could I ask You for one more?*

"Your pride's goin' to end up freezing Noah into an icicle if you don't fess up soon." Mama tapped her foot on the wooden floor.

Abigail stood up and spun around to face her mama. Before she could talk herself out of it, she blurted out. "I'm. . .I'm. . .sorry Mama for sassing."

"Daughter, what are you waiting on? Go let that man

inside."

She rushed past her, not waiting for her to say anything else. On her way out of the kitchen, Abigail stopped to grab the two dish towels hanging on the stove. Might need 'em to clean up the mess he makes on his way in the house. *Mama won't like him carrying in all of winter with him.*

As she reached the front door, Abigail threw it wide open and bellowed, "Hurry up and get in here. You must be chilled to the bone."

"T-thank you." Noah shook the remnants of the snow off of his overcoat and stomped his boots on the porch before he came in.

Abigail slammed the door behind him and shivered from the frigid temperatures they'd let inside. After she moved a smaller rug from the dining room, Abby told Noah to stand on it. She handed him one of the towels she'd brought with her, and then went into the parlor to start a fire in the hearth to get the place warmed up.

She scurried back to where the mercantile owner stood and leaned over to wipe up the drips his woolen coat left on the plank floor. After she finished, she said, "Mr. Presley, I believe you brought half of the precipitation in with you." Abigail swatted his arm with the soggy towel in her hand.

"The hot cocoa is ready," Mama said.

Abigail jumped at her mother's announcement and she wondered why she always seemed to come in at just the right moment.

"Daughter, if you don't hurry, this young man will catch a death of cold." Mama stopped and glanced at Abigail, her eyes filling with tears. She turned and hurried out of the room.

A Texas-size lump formed in Abigail's throat. Words couldn't make their way around it if she wanted them to. Tears threatened to pour down her own cheeks as she thought of her papa. She finished cleaning the floor and started to move the rug, but Noah took hold of it and placed it near the dining room door.

"Thank you, Mr. Presley."

"You're welcome and you've probably figured out, since I'm here, that we're not having church today. Pastor Blair put out a sign. Saw it when I headed over here." Noah smiled. "Oh, how I wanted to hear you sing."

"Oh, I'm sure you and all of Central City would have, too." Abby appreciated Noah for changing the subject. Any more of a mention of Mama's earlier comment needed swept under the rug he just put away. She couldn't imagine ever thinking that the man her heart was smitten with would succumb to the same fate as her papa.

Fifteen

"The cocoa's getting cold." Noah heard Mrs. Thompson's reminder. "What is taking you two so long? Get yourself in here."

"Guess we better get in there before she throws it all away." Abigail grabbed Noah's arm and they scooted down the long hallway into the toasty kitchen.

Noah saw Mrs. Thompson standing near the stove, stirring the chocolate, sugar and milk mixture. She took it off the burner and poured the steaming cocoa into three mugs on the oak table in the middle of the room.

"Son, what on earth were you thinking? You could have died out there in one of those snow drifts. Why don't you take off your boots and your socks? We need to put them over near the fire to dry them out."

Noah raised up his hands. "Mrs. Thompson don't you worry. My boots are just fine. I'm fine."

"Mr. Presley, you look like a drowned rat. I'm not going to have you catching something. Here, move over closer to the hearth."

Before Abigail's mother grabbed the chair out from under him, Noah moved near the fire.

"There, I feel better. You'll be dry in no time. Now, if you two don't mind, I'm going upstairs. I feel I need to rest."

"Mama, you go on. I'll take care of things down here."

Abigail's mother picked up her cup and headed toward the door, and then turned and walked over to Noah. "Mr. Presley, thank you for clearing our walk this morning. Without a man in the house now..." She stepped back and nodded at him before she turned and walked out of the room.

"Glad to help, Mrs. Thompson."

After the woman left, he grabbed one of the mugs and sat down on the bench at the table. Abigail took the other cup and instead of joining him, she put it down close to the wash basin. Noah watched her busy herself at tidying up the immaculate kitchen.

Not wanting to stare at his kitchen companion, he kept his eyes focused on his hands wrapped around the warm cup. His body still ached from the cold and he questioned if he'd ever regain the feeling in his toes or fingertips. The fire helped and at the moment sitting in the same room as Abigail warmed his heart and the hot cocoa made his hands toasty.

"Mr. Presley, Mama made this pound cake to take for Homecoming Sunday, would you like a piece to go with your cocoa?"

"If you're sure your mother won't mind; I'd love a slice."

Abigail stopped flittering around long enough to cut him a huge piece of cake, which covered the entire plate she handed him. He noticed her slice was a mere sliver of his. She then poured more of the steaming sweetness for both of them and sat down to join him at the rectangular table.

As she took her place across from him, Noah lifted his mug and took a big swig out of it. Immediately he regretted the decision and wanted to spit the hot cocoa back in his cup. He'd forgotten she'd just poured it right from the stove. Noah swallowed and the richness burned all the way to his toes.

"Mr. Presley, you might want to let the cocoa cool a bit before you drink it next time."

"Thanks. Next time you might want to warn me sooner before I char my entire insides." Noah smiled at her as he stabbed his fork into the generous slice of cake, coming up with a hefty size bite he put in his mouth. "So is it true? Is your grandfather coming to Central City?"

"What? I didn't hear a word you said. Didn't your mama teach you not to talk with your mouth full?"

Noah took a couple of small sips from his mug before he spoke again. "Sorry. Yes, she tried. Must have forgotten I'm eating with a woman. Normally it's my brother and my pop. They don't care about etiquette."

"Now what were you saying?"

"I heard your grandfather is coming to Central City? But with this snow, I think he'll be delayed a few days."

"How did you know Mama contacted him?"

"Mrs. Collins said she heard—"

"Well, is that so." Abigail stood up from the table and put her hands on her hips. "And, Mr. Presley, where did the town's busy body hear this piece of gossip?"

"Ah, well…" Noah hemmed and hawed, not sure what to say. He'd already implicated his employee when he blurted out her name and he could tell Abigail's questions would take him down a road he didn't want to go on.

"How convenient for you that Mrs. Gossip has a direct line to the telegraph office. You don't have to wait for Mr.

Collins to come in for coffee now to hear the latest."

Oh, Lord in heaven, this isn't going well.

Noah took a few deep breaths. "Miss Thompson, let me start over. Please?"

"I wish you would."

For the next five minutes he filled Abigail in on the tidbit of information he overheard from his employee. "Trust me, after I heard her I had quite the discussion with Edna Mae Blabber Mou—" Noah couldn't believe what he'd just said. He'd used Mrs. Collins God-given name and the exact name he only uttered to himself when she got him riled up.

"Mr. Presley, I do declare."

"Sorry," Noah clipped off the apology. So far today his talking had dug him into quite a hole and if he said more it might swallow all six foot of him. He couldn't figure it out, but every time he got close to Abigail Thompson his tongue flapped and fluttered. She completely unnerved the tarnation out of him.

He glanced over at her before his eyes returned to pondering his ragged cuticles. *Was that a smile curling her pretty lips? No, I'm certain she thinks I'm a cad.*

Silence blanketed the kitchen as if winter had settled inside the stately Victorian, too. More words eluded Noah and the expression on Abigail's face told him he better finish his cocoa and skedaddle pretty quick.

He took matters into his own hands and announced, "Thank you, I'll be on my way." Noah stood and placed his Stetson back on his head. "Miss Thompson, I'm truly sorry for overstepping. I shouldn't have gossiped."

"Mr. Presley, I accept your apology. You've explained yourself and how you knew. The truth is, I don't want to move, but Mama and Gramps are gonna do whatever they choose. And I won't have anything to say in the mat—"

Abigail let out a wail that almost knocked Noah's hat right back off of his head. Her hands shot up to her face and a flood of tears streamed out between her fingers.

Noah raced over to her side, but didn't have a clue what to do. And nothing popped into his head on the way over to her, either. He reached his hand out to touch her arm, and then decided to pat her shoulder. A safer area. Not sure what else to do, he stood next to her, waiting for heaven knows what.

Abigail pulled her hand away from her face and smiled at Noah. She turned and his arm brushed her back. Before he knew what happened, his arm wrapped around her shoulder and she melted into his side. *If I die at this very moment, I'm a happy man.*

He patted the top of her head and Abigail's blond curls bounced. Her tears settled down to an occasional sniff, so he offered her his handkerchief.

"Thank you again." Abby stepped back from Noah and wiped her nose. He couldn't help but notice a difference in her expression. She now wore a determined look on her tear stained face. "Mr. Presley, I've decided no one's goin' make me go back to Dallas. Not Mama or Gramps. I'm staying right where God put me."

"Well, Miss, sounds like you've made up your mind." He smiled and realized he liked Abigail Thompson's feistiness – especially if it helped her stay in Central City.

"Guess I better get back to the mercantile." Noah tipped his hat as he headed to the Thompson's front door.

Abigail closed the front door behind Noah, but peeked out of the curtain to watch him trudge up the walk he'd shoveled earlier. He glanced back at the house and she couldn't help but notice his smile still lit up his handsome face. Abby swooned at getting to see his best feature again. She loved his cute dimple etched in his right cheek.

Footsteps on the wooden floor behind Abigail startled her out of her dream. She turned around and couldn't help but see her mama's swollen eyes.

"Mama, what's the matter?" Abby hurried to her mother's side and put her arms around her.

"Just remembering, daughter. Just remembering." Mama raised her hand and put it on Abigail's cheek. "It looks as if you've been doing a little crying yourself this morning."

"Oh, it's nothing." She didn't want to disclose the tantrum she had in front of Noah. Her mama didn't need to know the reason for her red eyes.

"Abigail, let's brew up some tea, and then go sit and talk some in the parlor. We'll be warmer in there."

What does Mama want to talk about now? I already said I was sorry. Abigail followed her mama back into the kitchen and watched as she filled the tea kettle. Her mother put a measure of tea leaves in the water to boil on the stove.

Minutes later, the whistle on top of the tea kettle sounded. Abigail took a piece of cheese cloth out of the drawer next to the stove and placed it over the spout to keep the leaves from spilling into the china cup. Mama broke out the special company cookies and placed a plate of them on the tray, which Abby carried back down the hall to the parlor.

"A special treat for us since we're stuck inside." Mama sat down on the settee.

"Another one? Mama, we've already had cocoa. Remember?" Abigail chuckled. She poured her mother a cup of tea and put a few cookies onto the saucer. The plate of cookies she left on the side table.

Abby filled her cup and grabbed a couple of the date filled tarts before sitting next to her mama. She knew she should tell her she'd already consumed a sliver of cake during Mr. Presley's visit, but kept the news to herself. No use spoiling another opportunity for something sweet.

The fire in the hearth crackled, sending up sparks into the chimney. Abigail savored the cookies and the warmth from the fire. Both began to sooth her weary soul. Her mama seemed content. She thought maybe she'd forgotten what she wanted to talk to Abigail about. If it had to do with moving away from Colorado, Abby wouldn't worry about it tonight. Tomorrow she'd start making her plans to stay in Central City.

"Daughter." Mama paused. She seemed she needed to collect a lost thought. "Dear, I believe Mr. Presley has taken a real shine to you. And I can tell the feelings are mutual."

Abby's teacup stopped in mid-air and if she didn't know any better, her breathing halted for a moment. She also didn't need anyone to tell her that the color rose on her cheeks. Clear from her lace collar to her forehead.

"Well, daughter, are we in agreement?" Her mother smiled and took a drink of tea.

"Mama, Mama, Mama. Mr. Presley is well meaning toward us purely for Papa's sake. Nothing more, nothing less." Abigail gulped the rest of her tea and shoved a cookie in her mouth so she'd have time to think of something else to say if her mother asked.

"Abigail, you must be blind if you haven't seen this young man's intentions. I realize he's been kind to come after your father passed, but today Noah Presley almost froze to death. He knew we didn't have a reason to venture out and he still shoveled through waist high snow. He did it because he's taken with you, dear."

Noah did seem interested, but she was mourning the loss of her papa. Societal customs wouldn't allow her to court anyone in the year to follow. Noah Presley wouldn't wait around for her and anyway, if her mama and Gramps had their way she'd return to Dallas to marry someone else.

"But, Mama, I only want to marry Noah," Abigail didn't realize she'd spoken the words out loud until she heard her mother's gasp.

Sixteen

"Pray tell, women. I will never understand 'em," Noah's words echoed off the newly fallen snow as he made his way back to the mercantile. "And, Lord, I believe Miss Abigail flat perplexes the socks off of me."

Noah stomped his feet on the wooden planks outside of his store and used the broom to brush off the rest of the snow which accumulated on his boots. Didn't want to tramp any inside, Mrs. Collins would have his head when she came into work if he left a puddle or two. Looking over his shoulder, Noah wondered when he'd open for business again—thanks to the November blizzard.

"Good morning, Mr. Presley."

Noah almost lost his balance when he spun around to see who spoke to him. And who was as crazy as he was to get out on this messy morning.

"Samuel?"

"One and the same." The older fellow grinned. "Got some coffee brewing?"

"Sure do. Come on in." Noah held the door for the old timer and followed him into the warmth of Presley Mercantile.

Noah poured them both a hearty cup after it finished brewing and slid a cup across the counter where his friend sat on his usual bar stool.

"Son, I haven't seen this much snow since before you came into this world." Samuel took a swig of his coffee.

"Oh, you don't know what you're talking about. It's not been twenty-three years since we've seen this much snow. I remember the storm of '82. That one nearly buried the herd of cows up at Tompkins' farm."

"You know, you could be right, Noah, that one was a doozy."

"I think the Rocky Mountain News said we received thirty-six inches in less than eight hours on that one." Noah jumped up and went behind the counter to retrieve his ledger to make note of this storm, but when he leafed through the first few pages, he stopped. He'd grabbed the wrong book.

Noah stashed it back under the counter and said, "Samuel, "I'm penciling in my prediction." Noah opened his book to November four and wrote forty inches." He glanced over at Samuel and added. "That's until I get the exact amount, when the experts come up here to measure it."

"Yeah, when the fool gets out in this mess."

"Like us." Noah laughed at his friend.

"Like us two lunatics. And speaking of which." Samuel took another sip of his coffee. "I saw ya coming from the Thompson's house. Wasn't it a tad early to be visiting? Or are you getting an early start on courting Miss Abigail?"

Noah almost spit out his coffee when he heard Samuel's proclamation. "If it's any of your business, old man, I simply went over there to clear their walk."

Once the words tumbled out of Noah's mouth, they sounded as lame as a three-legged dog.

"Son, who are you kidding? Don't believe the two ladies were in dire need of going anywhere today. What do you think?"

Noah didn't have an answer and anything he did say would sound stupid. Wiping the counter seemed the thing to do and maybe the subject would disappear without any more comment.

"Since you're not answering, I'll take it that it's true and the subject's closed." Samuel stood up and walked over to retrieve his heavy wool jacket he'd hung on a hook near the stove.

Noah watched him put it on and head for the door, but then the man turned and faced him.

"With all this snow, I'm sure Mrs. Thompson's father will have some trouble getting here. I could tell she was pretty anxious for him to come to Central City with the words she included in the telegram she sent him." He proceeded to tell Noah what the note said.

Noah nodded, surprised at Samuel's disclosure. Normally the telegrapher was closed mouthed about his telegrams, leaving any such spreading to his wife. But today he sang like a canary implementing a friend in the crime of the century.

"Mr. Samuel Collins, I can't believe what I just heard come out of your mouth." Mrs. Collins stood next to the curtain to the back room. Her loud voice caused both men to spin around and stare at the older woman.

"Ed. . .Edna Mae what on earth. . .are you. . .doing here?" Samuel sputtered out the question. His face blushed clear up over his bald head.

"Obviously watching a grown man flapping his chops

about something that is none of Mr. Presley's business."

Noah would have laughed out loud at the absurdity of her statement, but decided she didn't look like she thought any of this was humorous.

"Mrs. Collins, honestly he didn't tell me anything I didn't already know." Noah watched the town gossip's eyebrows tweak a tad. "Yes, I visited the Thompson's this morning. Miss Abigail told me what her mama said in the telegram."

"Oh, she did, did she?" The woman tapped her finger to her cheek as if contemplating what to say next. "Pray tell, Mr. Presley, what were you doing traipsing through all this snow calling on that pretty young lady at such an early hour?"

Noah felt himself blushing like his old friend. *How did we get on the subject of me? I liked it better when Samuel was in the dog house.*

"Dear, wait till you hear this. Noah, here, was being a Good Samaritan. He told me he went over simply to shovel their walk. Nothing else. Guess he thought they might want to go on up to church later today. Maybe for evening service—that's if we were having it." Samuel's raucous laughter filled the quiet mercantile. He seemed to enjoy the shift in attention from him.

Noah noticed Mrs. Collins eyes lit up and he could almost see her mind clanking out what she would tell anyone who would listen. News this big wouldn't take long to get around the tiny town. Edna Mae would spread it as fast as her short, chubby legs would carry her around and through the snow drifts.

Abigail's hand shot up to her mouth. "Mama, did I just say I wanted to marry Mr. Presley?"

"Yes dear, you did." Her mother's expression seemed none too pleased with Abigail's admission of true love. "And, daughter, how do you propose to do that when you live in Texas?"

"We'll see about that." Abby stood up after her curt remark. Her sudden movement made her almost spill the last of her tea unto her lap. "Mama, I'm going to clean up the dishes and go on to my room. I've got some reading to do and I'm behind in writing in my journal."

"Daughter, I don't know what I'm going to do with you, but you'd do well to straighten up. Now, let me help you with the dishes."

"No, stay right there. I'll do them."

Abigail walked out of the parlor with all the dishes and headed into the kitchen. A few swishes in the hot water on the stove and she'd be done. Then her plan would begin. She had no intention of going up to her room to read or write, for that matter. The only thing on Abigail's mind at the moment—Presley Mercantile. Noah would help her come up with a strategy on getting her to stay in Colorado.

With the last dish put away, Abigail headed for the back door. Thank goodness she'd put on her papa's trousers under her wool skirt and Mama had moved Papa's work coat to the end peg. She'd look like someone that the cat drug in, but she'd be warm on her way to see Mr. Presley.

Careful not to let the door squeak, Abby opened it slow and easy. *So far, so good.* When she'd made her exit, she shut the door. There was one problem; she stepped into the snow and lots of it. "Great. I guess I should have escaped out the front where Noah shoveled."

Thank goodness the drifts on the south side of the house

weren't as high as on the north. This gave Abigail less of the white stuff to maneuver over. By the time she reached the front of the house she wanted to give up and go back inside, but she trudged across the street to the mercantile.

Lights inside the store lifted her spirits. Abigail tried the door, but nothing happened. She tried again, but it still didn't move. *Since it's Sunday, Noah's probably in the storeroom doing whatever he does and doesn't hear—*

"Miss Abigail Thompson, what are you doing out in this mess?" Mrs. Collins asked as she opened the door.

I could ask you the same thing. "Oh, I'm just out for a morning stroll." Abigail shivered, hoping the woman would move aside soon so she could get inside the mercantile before she froze solid.

"Edna Mae, let the poor child in. Can't you see her teeth are chattering?"

The older woman glanced over her shoulder to the person speaking. Abigail could only imagine the look she gave her husband. She'd recognized the telegrapher's voice from other visits to the store.

Finally, Mrs. Collins moved and Abby rushed in and headed right over to the fire. She danced on one foot, and then the other, hoping the feeling would return to them before she tried to walk over and get some warm coffee.

Seventeen

Abigail could feel Mr. Presley and Mr. and Mrs. Collins' eyes boring into her back while she stood warming herself next to the fire. Why were those two here? She needed to talk to Noah.

"Here's a towel for you, Miss Thompson." Noah smiled as he walked over to her. "I get the privilege this time of drying you off." Noah stopped and Abigail wasn't sure but the look on his face and the shade of red he turned told her he thought he'd been completely inappropriate. The sad part, he had an audience to witness his blunder.

She felt sorry for him, but she couldn't help but see the humor in it all. Abigail patted his arm and let a little chuckle slip out. "Mr. Presley, you're fine. I can dry myself off without assistance. You tend to the floor and all will be cleaned up in no time."

"Thanks."

Abigail dried off and when she stepped away from the stove, she could actually move her fingers and toes again.

Abby didn't realize that such a short walk could almost turn a person's blood into instant icicles, but she did now.

"Girl, come over here and get yourself some coffee," Mrs. Collins tapped the counter and pointed at the seat next to her husband. "You sit there next to the old coot. He won't bite you."

"Oh, I don't know, Edna. You didn't fix me breakfast this morning." Samuel Collins laughed.

"Don't believe a word he says. I fed him a hearty fare, but let a minute go by and he forgets he ate."

Abigail sipped her coffee and enjoyed watching the older couple. They reminded her of her parents and their exchanges of good-natured teasing. Sometimes they'd do it when she was around. Other times she'd catch them in pretending they argued, but they would laugh. Abby knew Mama and Papa and these two truly loved each other.

"Why the long face all of a sudden?" Noah said as he came up and stood next to her.

Abby released a sigh as she pondered her response. Then she said, "Sometimes things remind me of Papa and my heart smiles, but my face shows something else. My parents loved to tease each other and the Collins here acted like they once did."

"Oh darling, I'm so sorry. We didn't mean to bring hurting on you." Mrs. Collins came and put her arms around Abby. "Now, now. You'll be fine."

Abigail never knew a person's bosoms could act as a pillow and could begin to suffocate someone without the other knowing it, but if Mrs. Collins didn't let her go in a second, she was sure as dead.

"Edna Mae, if you don't release this poor girl, she's going to smother in there," Samuel stated exactly what Abby surmised.

The older woman did and Abigail could breathe again. She tried not to gasp for air, but she knew she did right after Mrs. Collins let her go.

"Dear, I'm sorry." Mrs. Collins' cheeks flushed pink. "Well I'm not doing anything right today. Samuel, maybe you and I need to leave before I do hurt someone."

Abigail wished Mr. and Mrs. Collins would leave the mercantile. She didn't have much time to discuss her plan with Noah. *Anyway, I'm still not sure why these two people are out in weather like this?*

"Edna Mae, you're probably right. We should be skedaddling out of here. Ah. . .I think I remember you telling me you wanted me to fix the wood stove."

"What are you talking about, Samuel? I didn't say anything about the wo—"

Samuel Collins grabbed his wife's arm, which stopped her from further conversation. Abigail heard the town gossip grumble as she was led toward the front door. Mrs. Collins shot her husband a look you could fry bacon on, and then it appeared something dawned on her and a smile broke out across her face.

"Yes, Mr. Collins, I do believe. . .yes, I think the wood stove needs fixin' 'cause it's mighty cold outside." Edna Mae undid her apron and flung it toward the counter.

The couple's playful exchange made Abigail chuckle, but then she realized what scheme they were brewing. Her cheeks burned and she could almost guarantee the bright color on her face matched Mrs. Collins apron. Noah's coloring didn't do much better. It went between pale and a light pink, but his cute dimple showed up and Abby smiled through her embarrassment.

She glanced over at the store owner and she could tell he

wanted to have a word with the couple, but they escaped out the door before he could say anything. He turned and said, "Miss Thompson, I don't know what I'm going to do with those two. I beg your pardon for their behavior."

"Oh you don't have to apologize, but know for sure I'll be the news around town by tomorrow. Mrs. Collins will fill people's ears about me visiting the mercantile while I'm in mourning. That'll spread like wildfire before this snowy day is written in the record books." Abigail moved over to the door and peered out. "And, I'm sure Mama will know I'm here before I get back to tell her so."

"You're right about that." Noah walked behind the counter and picked up the apron Mrs. Collins tossed on her way out of the store. "Now, miss, what is it that brings you out in this unexpected blizzard?"

"Well, Mr. Presley. There's...I'm..." Abigail stammered and wasn't sure how to broach the subject of asking for his help.

"What is it, Miss Thompson?" Noah questioned her as he fiddled with the hem of the flowered apron he held.

"Mr. Presley, since Papa died I've been praying and thinking on the perfect plan to keep Mama and me in Central City and I think I've figured it out. But I need your help." Abigail paused her proclamation to stir a sugar cube into her lukewarm coffee.

"I'm not sure what assistance I can give you with your grandfather on his way."

"Mr. Presley, with this enormous amount of snow it will delay his arrival, and give us more time to implement my brilliant plan." Abby took another sip of her coffee. "When Gramps arrives in Central City, he won't know what hit him. He'll have no other choice than to move here himself."

"What exactly are *we* going to do to keep all of you here?" Noah asked as he squatted down behind the counter to stash Edna's apron on one of the shelves.

"Well, for starters Mr. Presley, I want you to help me buy the opera house."

Abigail's words shocked Noah so much he jerked his head up and the top of his ear caught on a tack sticking out below the register.

"Ouch." Noah grabbed at his injured ear.

"Mr. Presley, are you alright?" Abigail hurried behind the counter, but stopped short before she bowled him over.

"I'm fine." He nodded as he stood up.

"Let me see for myself." Abigail stood on her tiptoes and peered up at him.

Noah had heard that females faint at the sight of blood and he couldn't imagine trying to stop his ear from bleeding and picking Abigail up off the floor at the same time. Noah watched for a reaction from her. None came.

Well, I guess blood isn't gushing all over the place or she'd be making more of a fuss. And, as Abigail's hand touched the side of Noah's face, shivers ran from the top of his blond hair to the bottom of his worn boots.

"Ah, Miss Thompson, I—"

"Noah, why is it when I get close to you that all you can do is sputter all over yourself?"

He backed up a few steps to regain his senses. He knew for certain the young and very attractive woman standing in front of him didn't have a clue she'd just captured his heart. And he knew he'd do whatever she asked to keep her right where she was. Even if it took helping her purchase the opera house he wanted for himself—with all of his heart.

"And while we're at it, Mr. Presley." Abigail stopped talking and stared at Noah. "Are you even listening to a word I said?"

Noah nodded at her, still dazed from her standing so close and her delicate touch on his cheek.

"Anyway, while we're at it, I think we need to start calling each other by our God-given names. Since you and me will be working together, that is."

"Miss Thompson, oh I mean Abigail, I haven't agreed to help you yet." Noah couldn't help but laugh at the young woman. Her sassiness never ceased to amaze him and her boldness almost took his breath away.

"If you don't help me, Noah, Gramps is sure to head us right back to Dallas. He'll probably have the conductor hold the train so we get back quick." Tears started to run down Abigail's cheeks again.

Noah watched and knew his teasing had brought them to the surface. "Abigail, please forgive me for laughing, but you surprised me. No, shock is more like it. I know you want to stay here, but the opera house. . .I don't know if I can help you because. . ."

"Because what?" Abigail interrupted Noah. "It seems pretty simple to me. Your father owns the rundown establishment. I'd think he'd be more than happy to rid himself of the monstrosity."

The words she spoke stabbed Noah right in the middle of his heart. *Oh, Abigail, if you only knew. Simple and Cyrus Presley don't go together. Nothing with Pop is simple.*

"Abigail, let's go over near the stove and I'll try and explain the situation, and then maybe you will understand what it is we're dealing with." Noah scooted the stools over close to the wood stove and Abigail sat down. He turned and grabbed a couple of logs and tossed them on the hot embers and sent up a prayer. *Father, I don't know how to tell her she might be too late. Help me say the right words.*

"Miss Abigail, nothing about this opera house is easy and especially asking my pop to sell it." Noah took a deep breath and continued. "You have to understand him, and our family, a little bit before dealing with him."

"How so?"

"Our family on Pop's side owned the Central City Opera House. Gram had me sitting on a piano bench long before my feet touched the pedals. Loved spending time there. But my father had no intention of keeping it after my grandmother died. When he sold it, he said, 'Too many memories.'"

"Funny thing, Abigail, he won it back five years ago in a poker game. For once in his life, Pop had a string of wins and a man named Stephen Cutler didn't. At the end of the evening, Mr. Cutler only held one thing of value and the last hand proved too much for his empty pockets. He had to sign over his last asset, the opera house, to my father."

"I can't believe he sold it after your grandmother passed, but with what you just said, he doesn't care about the old place. I'd think he'd be clamoring to get rid of the likes of this eye sore."

"You'd think so, but again nothing with my father is easy. After he acquired the opera house, he tried to sell it, again. But Jake Taylor, the banker, informed him the property came with a lien Cutler forgot to disclose. Pop would have to pay off the debt before he could sell it to anyone."

"Do you have any idea how much he owes?"

"Yes, but…" Noah didn't want to tell Abigail he wanted

to buy the opera house himself and had the monies to pay off the debt. Or worse, if his suspicions were correct, having to tell her that someone already had dibs on the place they both wanted. Those two things might make her leave the mercantile and go pack her own bags for Texas.

"Noah, what's the matter? You look like you've seen a ghost again."

"It's not that bad, Abigail. It's worse. Someone else has already put the money down to buy the opera house. I sort of accidentally found out about the plan a few weeks ago."

"Sort of *accidentally* found out? How do you do that, Noah?"

"By taking my father's ledger." Noah heard Abigail gasp. "There's more. Then I followed the banker into the opera house one night and overheard him and Matthew Tappen talking about the opera house and a JAR Corp. interested in buying it."

Abigail stood up so fast the stool she'd been sitting on fell over with a thud. She started to pace around the mercantile. "Noah Presley, you need to clean out your ears." Her tone and look she gave him could, at that moment, bring a team of horses to a screeching halt.

"I'm just telling you what I heard."

"Noah, it can't be. The company you just mentioned belongs to my grandfather. Why would he be trying to buy the opera house?"

"Not sure. All I know is I snuck into the opera house and almost died in the process. I overheard part of their plan. What I don't get is why they met there at such a strange hour, and without my pop? Unless there is something else going on."

"If someone is doing something shady, my grandfather isn't involved and will get to the bottom of whatever it is when he arrives in Central City."

"Miss Thompson, it's beginning to sound like we've got a mystery on our hands."

Eighteen

"Mystery?" Abigail stopped and planted her feet right in front of Noah and stared down at him. "I can't believe Gramps would. . ."

Noah waited for a moment for her to continue, but she didn't. She seemed lost in some far away thought. Her pacing began again. This time the heels of her boots made a quick, rhythmic sound on the wood planked floor as she waltzed around the mercantile.

"Abigail, I'm telling you what I heard. I'm afraid when your grandfather gets here, he won't be happy with what's going on."

The clicking of Abigail's heels stopped clear across the room and she spun around. "Noah, they have no idea who Jacob Reardon is. He's an honest businessman and wouldn't take to anyone trying to pull something over on him.

"Around Mama and me, Gramps is a gentle spirit, but when you deal with him in business, well, Katy bar the door. Mr. Presley, we have to find out what is going on before my grandfather gets here."

"There is something else, Abigail." Noah rose from the stool and walked behind the counter. He picked up Pop's invoice book and leafed through the first few months of the year, stopping on the month of August. "There are some entries I want to show you."

Abigail came over and joined him and the two of them looked at the ledger pages. Noah pointed to the line registered as a payment received with the name of JAR Corp. written next to it. Without a word, he turned the page and showed Abigail two more entries.

"Oh, Noah, it is Gramps. What are we going to do?"

"I'm not sure what *we* are going to do, but a couple ideas are kicking around in my head, But..." Noah leaned down and hid the ledger back under the counter.

"But, what?" Abigail inquired as she plopped herself on the lone bar stool in front of the counter.

"Abigail, I don't want you involved. This could get dangerous."

"If you hadn't noticed, Mr. Presley, I'm already in it because of Gramps."

"Hey, maybe he and your papa have been in cahoots on buying the opera house. Do you think your grandfather decided to finish the deal to keep you and your mama here?" Noah's thought popped out before he had time to catch it. He felt a smile creeping up and his heart suddenly lifted. He could almost hear a choir of angels singing.

"Noah, I don't know, but knowing Gramps, he's been keeping an eye on us since we got here. Even more after Papa died." Abigail went and grabbed their two coffee cups and poured each of them another cup. "Now since we are working together on this, there's no time like the present to get started."

"Miss Thompson, just to let you know, I still haven't told you that I'm working with you. Right now I'm not certain this isn't something more than what we need to mess with. I think we need to talk to Sheriff Devoe before we get too involved."

"After what you've told me, you and I are working together. Whether you like it or not. Now where did you put that ledger?" Abigail jumped up from the stool and headed toward Noah.

"Whoa, Nellie."

"What?"

"If you haven't noticed, you've been here for two hours and I'm sure your mama's figured out you're not hiding out in your room."

"But. . ."

"No buts about it, Abigail. If we're going to be a team." Noah smiled. "You're going to have to rein in your enthusiasm." Again, his word choice didn't come out right.

"I beg your pardon."

"Guess that came out a little harsh. Sorry. For today, let me escort you home and when the snow thaws we'll get back together. Meanwhile, each of us will try and find out what's going on."

"Any suggestions on how we're supposed to do that?" Abigail began tapping her foot. Impatience showed mightily on her pretty face.

"First of all we need to pray and, if you can, without giving it away, talk to your mama. See if she knows anything. Maybe, look in your father's files. Something could show up where we least expect it." Noah held the coat Abigail wore in and she slipped into the woolen garment. Her long blond curls nestled themselves under the corduroy collar.

"I don't know, Noah. Oh I mean, partner. Maybe you need

to talk to Mama about what she may know."

"No, I believe that's your job." Noah laughed as he opened the mercantile door. As he stepped aside to let Abigail pass, she loosed the curls her collar had held captive. All of him wanted to reach out and touch the silky tresses, but logic told him to keep his hands to himself. And, knowing Abigail Thompson, she might haul off and slap him.

Neither spoke as they trudged across the snow packed streets of Central City. Not another soul meandered around the tiny town. Noah, again, wondered what had possessed him that morning to go out in the aftermath of the snowstorm. Then he remembered the very reason and she strolled right next to him as they headed to her stately Victorian home. The one she'd have to sneak back into so her mama would be none the wiser.

"Abigail, you know we can't say anything to anyone about this," Noah whispered the words with as much meaning as he could muster since he was so cold.

"I won't, but I'm not sure Mrs. Busybody hasn't gotten the word out about me spending half the day at the mercantile today."

"Edna Collins is the least of our worries." Noah answered as he opened the back screen door for Abigail. "Now you best get inside before your mama catches you." He tipped his hat and turned to head back to the mercantile, but changed his mind. "Abigail?"

"Yes."

She stood on the bottom stair looking up at him as if waiting for him to disclose a hidden secret. He couldn't resist the urge and if she slapped him, so be it. He reached down and kissed her cheek, and then stole away to the side of the Victorian.

Noah wasn't sure but he thought he heard her giggle,

which made him smile until he eyed Mrs. Thompson on the front porch. *Please, please, please don't notice me.*

"Mr. Presley, pray tell what are you doing out here? You've spent more time out in this weather than any sensible human being ever should," Abigail's mother yelled from her front porch.

Noah didn't have an intelligent answer to her question. Never one to be quick on his feet when something or someone threw him off guard, especially after kissing her daughter five seconds before.

"Well, son. You gonna answer me before we both freeze to death standing out here?"

"Ah, ma'am, I guess you could say I'm out for my late afternoon stroll," Noah knew what he said wouldn't convince anyone with half a brain, but he wanted to give Abigail time to get inside and out of her coat. "Mrs. Thompson, actually, it's not too bad out here."

"Son, you must have been born in a barn. Nobody in their right mind could enjoy this ungodly weather. Now you better get yourself home."

"Will do, ma'am. Now you have a fine day." Noah hurried down the street to the mercantile. While he stood at the pot belly stove and unthawed his frozen fingers and toes, he prayed a prayer that Abigail got inside and upstairs before her mama caught sight of her.

"Keep her talking, Noah," Abigail said as she tore at her jacket. The wool of the coat fought with the lace on the sleeve of her blouse. She tugged and pulled and finally got her arms loose and the garment lay in a heap, inside out, at her feet.

"Abigail, what are you doing in there?" Her mama's question coming down the hallway made her snatch up the disheveled item and finished rearranging its sleeves. Just at the nick of time, Abigail opened the wardrobe near the back door and tossed the coat inside. With her heart beating at a steady rate against her chest, she closed the door quietly, leaving all of the evidence behind. Her hand touched where Noah kissed her.

"Daughter, I ask you again. What on earth are you doing? You look like you've been in a ruckus and the other person won." Mama fashioned Abigail's curls back up with some pins from the pocket of her striped apron.

"Thank you."

Her mother stared at Abigail a minute, and then said. "Oh never mind what I'm thinking. Anyway, with you, dear, I quit being surprised about what you do when you turned about five years old."

Thank You, Thank You, Thank You, Lord.

Her mama turned and walked back down the hallway and Abigail followed her to the parlor. On the way she decided to sway her mama toward one of the subjects she loved to talk about. Her father. Maybe Abigail could learn some valuable information.

"Mama, do you think that this snow today is going to delay Gramps from getting here?" Abigail watched her mama's eyes light up at the mention of him, but then she turned and gave her one of her sideway glances.

"We'll see, as far as I'm concerned he can't get here soon enough."

Abby ignored her mama's comment and babbled on. "I can't wait until he comes either. We can go out and ride. I know Dancer has missed it. And Herkimer, when I went over there the other day, is itching to get out there, too"

From the look on her mama's face, her incessant talking confounded her. For whatever reason Abby couldn't get her tongue to quit wagging. "Mama, I just know Gramps is going to love Central City."

This statement brought a blank stare from her mama and Abigail knew she wanted to say something, but remained silent.

"Mama, are you alright?"

"Yes, and I'm certain he won't *love* a thing about this place. After he sees all this snow," Abigail's mother pointed out of the parlor window, "he will have us on the next train."

Not with what Noah told me earlier, Mama.

"However, dear, part of his telegram should make you happy. Gramps said the business he had to finish up here would take him a while, but for us not to fret. He'd get us out of here as quick as he could." Mama smiled and gathered up her sewing on her lap.

"We'll see about that," Abigail covered her mouth to muffle the words.

Her mother put her needle into the linen and glanced up at Abigail. "Daughter, what are you muttering about?"

"Nothing, Mama. Nothing at all." She didn't want to give anything away, but curiosity got the best of Abigail and she blurted out, "Did Gramps say anything else? Did he say…" She couldn't think of anything, and then her favorite candy popped into her head. "Mama, did he say he was bringing us some peppermint sticks?" *Abby, you could have been more creative.*

The mention of her most favorite things in the world, beside her papa, the Rocky Mountains and Herkimer, started her mouthwatering. Papa used to bring her the two treats when he returned from the courthouse in the evening.

"No, he didn't say anything about bringing your candy, but I did forget to tell you he said he had a surprise for us when he gets here. Wonder what Gramps has up his sleeve?

Abigail almost had to catch herself from falling over when her mama said those words and laughter tickled her insides. Oh how she wanted to giggle, but knew she'd have too much explaining to do if she did.

Oh, Mama, when Gramps gets to town you're in for a big surprise.

Nineteen

"What is all that racket?" Noah asked as he flung the curtain open between the store room and the front of the mercantile.

"Shush, Mr. Presley, can't you see I've got enough rattling me this morning?" Mrs. Collins sat on the floor of the mercantile, collecting the assorted nails and screws scattered around her. "Before you ask, the bottom fell out of the box when I moved it to clean."

Noah wanted to laugh, but decided instead to grab some empty jars off the back shelf and help her pick up the mess.

"So, Mr. Presley. . ." Mrs. Collins paused between handfuls. "I noticed you walked Miss Abigail home kinda late yesterday afternoon." She reached up and took the container Noah offered her.

He cleared his throat. "Thought it was the gentlemanly thing to do." Noah sat down on the floor and started picking up the nails and screws, and then dropped them into the jar sitting next to his knee.

"I'm not sure Mrs. Thompson would approve of such behavior. That is if she even knew her daughter slipped out and came over here."

At that moment Noah wanted to tell Edna Mae Collins to mind her own business, but decided he'd curb his response to the town gossip and said, "Ma'am, I'm certain Mrs. Thompson is aware of her daughter's comings and goings."

"I wouldn't be so sure. I've heard things. Oh my, I better shush up," Mrs. Collins stated as she put the last of the hardware in the jar next to her. She then attempted to stand, but lost her balance, landing on her backside.

Noah jumped up and reached for her, but realized too late that he didn't plant his feet first. When he heaved, she hoed and both of them sprawled across the wooden floor. Legs, arms and cotton material from the older woman's skirt and petticoat wrapped itself around the pair. Luckily, as far as Noah could tell, the predicament didn't reveal Edna Mae's where-with-alls for God and the whole world to see. When they finally uprighted themselves to a sitting position the bell on the door chimed.

"Well, it looks like you two are getting into your job," Samuel Collins commented after shutting the front door behind him.

"Shut up and get over and help us." Mrs. Collins fumed.

"Samuel, stay right where you are. If you get mixed up in this, somebody's bound to have to rescue all of us." Noah untangled his long legs from the folds of fabric and twisted his hip around to finally stand again. "Here, Mrs. Collins, let me help you."

"No, son, you've done enough. Samuel, get over here."

The woman's husband ran over and did as he was told and successfully brought his wife to a standing position. "There you go, dear. So, Noah, where's my coffee?" Mr. Collins smiled as he came over and sat on his stool.

"It's coming right up." Noah went over to start brewing the morning coffee. He moved around a little to make sure he hadn't broken anything then he thought he better be polite and asked. "Mrs. Collins how are you faring from our tumble?"

"Fair to middling." The woman took the dishrag and wiped up the counter after Noah moved away. "I'm sure I'll live."

"I hope so, dear. What would Noah do without you at the mercantile?" Samuel chuckled.

"Exactly. What would I do?" Noah interjected as he watched the older woman pick up the jars the two of them filled. But deep in his heart he'd like to find out how he'd do without her, even for a couple of days. His ears tired of her chattering.

"Well, it's nice to finally be appreci…" her words trailed off.

"Edna Mae, what on earth are you staring at?"

"Oh, it's the Thompson girl, Samuel. She's heading up the street and I sure hope when her grandfather gets here he can do something about her chasing all over the place." Frustration showed on Mrs. Collins face.

"Edna Mae, leave her be. She's young. And mighty pretty, if I might add." Samuel winked in Noah's direction. "If you'd be still, you'd have noticed someone in this room has taken a fancy to our Miss Thompson."

"Mr. Samuel Collins, I've noticed. That's all fine and good. I'm all for love blooming. But I personally think she need not to come in here alone. That's all I'm saying." Edna Mae picked up the broom and started to sweep, causing dust to fly everywhere. "But, mark my word, from what I deciphered in her grandfather's telegram, Mr. Reardon isn't…"

Mrs. Collins stopped and stared at her husband. Her hand flew to her mouth and in a split second she looked as if she'd seen a gaggle of goblins.

"Edna Mae, I do declare. You've gossiped your very last time," Samuel's loud baritone voice announced as he stood and took his wife's elbow and led her out the door of the mercantile.

As they made their way out, Noah heard her saying "But, Samuel, you left it there for the whole world to see."

Noah chuckled as he closed the door and picked up the broom to finish the job Edna left in the middle of the floor. "Well, my dear it looks like your days of gossiping are over and it's high time that miracle happened."

He turned to head to the store room, but stopped to glance out the window. "Guess I'm going to find out what it's like without you helping me today. And, I sure hope Abigail decides to come visit me on her way home. We've got some talking to do."

Abigail trudged up the steps of the yellow Victorian. Her trip to town didn't include a stop at the mercantile, even if she wanted to see Noah. Especially after she witnessed Mr. and Mrs. Collins coming out of there. Neither looked happy.

But she had to put that thought aside and her desire to visit the mercantile. Mama said she wanted the hot apple pie from Teller House. "Nothing more, Daughter. Come right home after you pick it up. Gramps will be here and we need to be ready to meet his train."

Abby hurried home and deposited the piping hot pie on

the counter and went up to dress in her Sunday best. Today, her grandfather would arrive in Central City and in less than an hour she'd kiss her second favorite person on earth, next to her papa. And, now maybe Noah. "Guess, then, I best hurry. Don't want to miss this special occasion."

"Daughter, are you about ready? Mr. Price is waiting out front for us."

Her mama's melodic voice rang out as Abigail opened her bedroom door. "Yes, I'm ready. Come on, Mama. Let's go."

Abigail raced down the stairs, two at a time and hit the bottom with a resounding thud. Her laughter sprang forth and she whirled around and smiled at her mama still halfway up the long staircase. Her sudden movement almost caused her to fall over.

"Daughter, if I could only trap half of the energy you display in your theatrics into music lessons we'd afford ourselves many hours of enjoyment."

Abby ignored her mama's comments and threw the front door wide open. The arctic chill filled the foyer and she realized she'd forgotten to put on her coat first. She closed the door and started toward the kitchen, but ran into her mama who came back carrying both their garments.

"Here, dear, you might want to put this on."

"Mama, what would I do without you?" The moment the statement left Abigail's lips, she regretted saying it. "Oh, my goodness. I didn't mean that to sound…" she decided to be quiet.

"I know you didn't. Let's hurry. Gramps will be at the train station and no one will be there to welcome him here."

Abigail threw on her coat and helped her mother with her scarf and the two waltzed out to the wagon waiting for them. Mr. Price sat holding the reins of his horse. The minute he saw

Abby and her mama the man hopped down and offered his help.

"You're so kind to do this for us." Mama stepped up into the wagon.

"No problem, ma'am. Miss Abigail mentioned your father coming to visit the other day and it's the least I can do." Mr. Price smiled at Abigail as he helped her up to sit next to her mama. He stepped in and took the reins. "Get going George, we have a train to meet."

Abby and her mama laughed as they headed up Main Street on their way to Eureka.

"Mr. Price, you really didn't name your horse George, did you?" Abigail couldn't help giggling at the older man.

"You bet, Miss Abby, and you want to know why I named him George?"

Abigail nodded, which made her ear muffs bob up and down on her head.

"Well, it's 'cause you and your papa took the names Herkimer and Dancer. They're the best I've heard around these parts."

Even though the mention of her father made her heart ache from missing him, she smiled since she couldn't agree more with Mr. Price's assessment. Again, Abby nodded, unable to speak around the lump in her throat.

They reached the train depot and Mr. Price helped each of them down. "I'll be here when you're ready." With that he climbed back up into his wagon.

"Thank you, again," Mama took Abigail's arm. "Father's train should arrive here any mom—"

The blast of the train whistle drowned out the last of Mama's sentence. Her mouth moved as if those around her could still hear every word she uttered.

"Come on, Mama. Hurry now. I think I just caught a glimpse of Gramps." Abigail grabbed her mother's arm and they took off towards the train.

As they neared the platform she spied him talking to a uniformed man. Gramps glanced up and smiled and that's all it took for Abigail to let go of her mama's arm and run to embrace her grandfather.

"Oh, I'm so glad you're here." Abigail hugged the older man's neck, not caring if others standing around gawked at her display of affection.

"Well, for goodness sakes, young lady." Gramps laughed as he stepped back. He took hold of Abigail's hand and squeezed. "Someone's happy to see me."

"Excuse me. There's *someone else* who missed you too." Mama squared her shoulders and tapped her foot on the platform.

Abigail spun around. She'd forgotten all about her mother, but she could tell Mama pretended seriousness. Without another word she went and hugged her father. Tears, mixed with chatter and smiles, filled the November chill.

"If I'd known I'd get this greeting, I'd have come sooner." Abigail's grandfather embraced Abigail and Mama again, and then they walked arm in arm to Joseph Price's wagon.

Twenty

Is it something I said? Noah questioned as he milled around his shop. First, Abigail hadn't stopped into the mercantile after Mrs. Collins spotted her the other day. Noah presumed her absence had to do with her grandfather's arrival from Philadelphia the same afternoon.

Second, and to make matters worse, he hadn't seen hide nor hair of Edna Mae Collins or Samuel since their exchange of words in the mercantile. This gossip thing had taken a serious turn in their household.

Four days without witnessing the older couple lovingly battling back and forth caused him a bit of concern, especially the part of Mr. Collins missing his morning coffee. "Think I'll make some extra, just in case he shows up today." Noah busied himself behind the counter, fixing his famous brew and praying for the pair.

"Lord, help this couple through their differences of opinion so they can get themselves back in here. I miss them." Noah glanced around his store at the chaos surrounding him.

"Oh, I never thought I'd hear myself say this, but it's Edna Mae I miss the most. Since she's been gone the mercantile has gone to pot."

The bell over the door chimed and Noah looked up. He hoped to see the now happy twosome strolling in, but instead caught a much more inviting sight. Miss Abigail Thompson sashayed in, stopping only a few feet from the counter he stood behind. His heart skipped a beat or two and, as usual, his mouth went dry.

"Good morning, Mr. Presley."

"Good morning, Miss Abigail," Noah replied after he regained his ability to talk and breathe at the same time, for which he was thankful. For some strange reason she seemed to always take his breath away when she came into any room.

"Mr. Pres— oh I mean Noah. I don't know why I have so much trouble remembering to use your God-given name. It's habit, I guess. Mama's upbringing is more worried about formality then friendliness. But, not me." To prove her point, Abigail pulled the wooden stool over closer to Noah and plopped herself down.

"Is that so?" Noah's voice squeaked out the three little words. They sounded as if he'd returned to puberty for a moment. Her nearness caused him to break out in a sweat. *Get control of yourself, man.*

"Noah Presley, are you listening to me?"

"Yes."

"Anyway, enough about our names. The main reason I stopped in, I wanted to find out what happened to Mr. and Mrs. Collins in here the other day."

"What's Edna Mae been flapping her chops about this time?" Noah could only guess the answer, but wanted to hear the latest goings on from Abigail's lips. He enjoyed her animation while telling her stories.

“Mrs. Collins isn’t saying anything. That’s what’s got me worried. I saw them when they both stormed out of here the other day and Samuel looked as mad as two dogs vying for the same bird.”

Noah’s sudden laughter filled the air. He didn’t mean for it to be so abrupt, but he couldn’t help it. The way Abigail phrased some things nearly tickled him to the soles of his leather boots.

“Pray tell, what are you laughing at?” Abigail turned toward him. “It’s not a laughing matter, Noah, the couple seemed in dire straits as they made their way up Main Street.”

The compassion written on her face melted his heart, so he brought his merriment to a halt. However, the urge to kiss her almost overwhelmed him. Instead of succumbing to the whim to do so, Noah told her what transpired with Edna Mae and Samuel. “Abigail, you should have seen her face when she realized she’d spilled the beans.”

“Serves her right. Nosing into Gramps’ business like that. Disgraceful. I bet Mr. Collins almost hit the roof.”

“Oh, he went well above the ceiling on her offence this time. I don’t think Central City will ever have to worry about Mrs. Collins telling another of her many tall tales ever again.”

“This is almost too good to be true, Noah. I can’t wait to tell Mama the news. She and the pastor’s wife have been praying for the Lord to get a hold of this woman’s tongue for as long as we’ve been in Colorado.”

Noah could only nod in agreement at the young woman’s comment. Anything else might have caused him to laugh out loud again. Or blurt out an unbecoming thought concerning her mother, which had just popped into his head.

What about the few times I’ve been the recipient of your

Mama's tongue lashing. Aren't we calling the kettle black here?

"Mr. Presley, is there a reason you're smiling? I continue to say I don't believe the subject of marital discourse is at all that funny."

"Neither do I." Embarrassed, Noah shifted his weight from one boot to the other. "Abigail, truly, this is a serious subject. I've been praying for Mr. and Mrs. Collins since the other day, too."

"So, is that what you were doing a few minutes ago when you were grinning all over yourself? You looked like your thoughts had high tailed you somewhere far from me and Presley Mercantile." Abigail smiled at Noah as she got up and headed over to the table stacked with wools and brocades.

As she attempted to lift one bolt of fabric, four slid off and landed on the wood floor with a bang, trapping her among the lot of them.

"Here, let me help you." Noah leapt from behind the counter and hurried to rescue her. Just as he went to grab Abigail's arm, she swayed out of his grasp.

"Oh goodness, oh. . .oh." Abigail teetered and plopped down hard on the various bolts, her feet still hidden under the stack.

Noah almost chuckled, but her expression told him otherwise. "Hold on. I've got an idea." He moved behind her and reached down and picked her up. As he went to sit her down, Abigail's blond curls tickled his nose. Fireworks exploded in his head and if he didn't breathe soon he'd lose consciousness.

"Mr. Presley, you can put me down now."

Noah gasped when he realized he still held Abigail to his chest. "Oh, Miss Thompson, I beg. . .oh, I'm so sorry." Noah let go of her and moved as far away as his boots could carry him. At that moment, no one needed to tell him his face glowed as bright as the noon day sun. "Truly, Miss Thompson, I beg your pardon."

Abigail stood next to the table and fidgeted with the lace on her sleeve. "Guess next time I shouldn't get myself into fixes I can't get myself out of, but thanks. I appreciate your help."

Noah nodded because any manner of speech escaped him. If he could speak, he wondered what he'd say to her to make amends for his behavior a moment before. But for now the memory of their closeness made his heart do somersaults in his chest and kept him tongue tied.

The ticking noise from the grandfather clock in the far corner broke the silence in the wood framed mercantile. Noah counted the seconds and as each passed he knew he needed to say something.

"I'm so sorry."

"Well, Mr. Presley, you should be." Abigail smiled at him as she moved around to the front of the table filled with material. "Noah, will you look at this mess. What do you say we finish cleaning up around here? See if we can *work* together."

"Remember, I haven't agreed with your proposition yet."

"Oh you will, Mr. Presley. You will. Now that Gramps is here. Anyway, back to the mercantile, do you know if Mrs. Collins is coming back?"

"No, but I sure hope so." Noah moved closer to Abigail and she looked up at him. He could see her hands trembling as she reached for a bolt of material. He took one off the pile and asked her when she hadn't moved, "Miss Thompson, are you waiting for something? You said we needed to get busy."

Together they tidied up the mounds of fabric and even put away some sewing notions Abigail found tucked between the piles. Noah tried his best to stay a foot or two away from the young woman and double checked his breathing on a few occasions.

"See that wasn't so bad. Finished in no time at all." Abigail snatched up her woolen jacket and headed for the door. "I gotta scoot. We'll work on our plan another day. I'm supposed to meet Gramps at the livery stable in a little while."

Noah noticed the sadness in her eyes before she looked down to brush off some threads that clung to her woolen skirt. *Did I cause this?* He hoped not, but it made him want to reach over and take her into his arms, erase whatever plagued her thoughts.

"Thanks, Abigail. I couldn't have cleaned this up without you," Noah opened the door for her, but instead of leaving, she lingered for a moment. Her hand reached up and touched his cheek.

"Noah, you're wel—"

"Well, well, well. What do we have here? Have I been replaced?"

Noah and Abigail spun around at the booming voice resonating from the front steps of the mercantile. None other than the town gossip stood three feet from them and Noah couldn't believe she'd witnessed everything. He wanted the earth to open up and swallow him whole.

But before God could answer his fervent prayer, Edna Mae Collins asked her question again. "Please tell me I can still work here, can't I?" The older woman dabbed at the corner of her eye.

Noah took a few deep breaths to get the wind back in his sails. Mrs. Collins' sudden appearance almost did him in.

Edna Mae, you couldn't have picked a worse time to come back to work.

"So can I?" she asked for a third time.

"Samuel does know about this, doesn't he?" Noah blurted out the question before his mind had sense to stop it. His curiosity got the best of him.

"Yes and Mr. Presley, he said he's sorry for taking me out of here so unceremoniously the other day. So, if you'll have me. I can start right away."

Noah gazed around the mercantile. Obviously he still needed her help. "Well, if Samuel says it's okay, so do I. Welcome back, Mrs. Collins."

The woman grabbed Noah and Abigail in an enthusiastic embrace and shouted, "These two love birds are together and I have my job back. I'm a happy lady." Laughter filled the mercantile.

Noah didn't dissuade the older woman's remark, but when Mrs. Collins turned from them, he stole a glance in Abigail's direction. Without a second thought, he winked at her. His cheeks heated up, but he didn't care. And the smile she gave him in return warmed his heart clear down to his ten toes.

Abigail escaped the older woman's strangle hold and took a few steps back. She'd never seen a woman so full of joy as Mrs. Collins. Baptists might forbid dancing, but today the town's busy body—or reformed one, she hoped—twirled around the perimeter of the fabric table as if someone wound her up tight.

"I don't mean to break up the party, but I have to go meet Gramps." With a wave of her hand, Abby exited the front door of the mercantile at just the exact moment tears decided to stream down her face.

"Oh, Lord, You have to help me," she sobbed out the words as she drew closer to the stable. Each step forward made her heart feel as if it would break in two at any second. Abigail stopped to lean on the building, trying to regain her composure, but fresh tears erupted every time she envisioned her gramps on the back of Dancer. Her papa's prized horse. "Lord, I don't know if I can do this. You're going to have to give me Your strength."

"Abigail, dear one, what's the matter?" Gramps rushed to her side, dropping the saddle he carried. He took Abigail into his arms.

"Gramps. . ." she spoke the single word, and then nestled into her grandfather's arms. Abigail envisioned this was how she'd feel resting in her heavenly Father's outstretched arms when she made her final journey home.

He wiped Abigail's tears away after a time, but didn't move away. Silence and the gentle wind played a melody around them as they stood together in the chill of the afternoon. For the first time since her Papa died Abigail knew the Lord had orchestrated the answer to her prayers. Peace, which passes all understanding, enveloped her soul.

Abigail raised her face to look up at her grandfather. "Gramps, I don't know about you but I think Herkimer and Dancer are ready for their ride."

"I think you're right, my dear. Let's get going before it's too late in the day to get some riding done."

They walked to the livery arm in arm. Abby chuckled as she watched Herkimer prance around his stall after she petted the side of his neck. Gramps saddled both of the horses and they started off on their ride.

"Are you ready, Gramps? Diggers Gulch is waiting."

Instead of answering Abigail's questions, her grandfather smiled and dug his heels into Dancer's side and took off chasing the wind.

"Guess he's ready. Come on Herkimer. We need to catch up. I need to show him the way to the gulch and the cemetery." Abigail raced off in the direction he went.

Thank You Lord for Your peace and for Gramps and his love for Mama and me. Now, could you help me catch up to him before he goes and gets himself lost.

Twenty-One

Noah didn't know much about women, but they sure did befuddle him. Especially Abigail Thompson. Today she completely confused him. He thought she came in to talk to him about her plan, but ended up helping him clean up the disheveled mercantile. Then she leaves with a wave and the saddest look he'd ever seen on a pretty little face like hers.

"Mr. Presley, I know you're fawning over Miss Abigail, but there's work to be done." Mrs. Collins swiped the side of his leg with the broom when she came up next to him.

He glanced down at the woman and crossed his arms. "I am doing no such thing. Miss Thompson is merely a friend. Nothing more."

Edna Mae let go of a chuckle that sounded like a couple of hens cackling before she continued. "Well, whatever she is to you—you've been standing at that window gaping out at her for the past ten minutes."

"I have not. I've been tidying up the mercantile." Noah gestured with his right arm the handy work, which he couldn't even see, but in the process he almost took out the older woman's head as his arm moved back to the right. "Sorry, Mrs. Collins."

"It's alright, son. Maybe you flapping your arms dusted a little. Didn't do much else. Other than mussing my hair some." She smiled at Noah as she took a glance into the mirror. After she put herself back together, she turned to Noah. "You are pulling my leg. You ain't done a thing except stare after that pretty young thing. Admit that she's got a hold of your heart."

Oh, and I'm going to tell you, the town gossip, how I feel about Abigail. Over my dead body that'll happen. Anyway, there's really nothing to tell.

And as if she read his thoughts, she came back with, "Come on, Mr. Presley, it's not like spilling the beans is going to kill you. You can tell me, I'll keep it a secret. Trust me, I'm a changed woman."

"I'm sure you are reformed, Mrs. Collins, but truly there is nothing to say on the subject." Noah left his post by the front door and walked across the mercantile to pour himself a cup of coffee.

"If you want to keep it all bottled up inside of you, that's just fine." Mrs. Collins leaned over to sweep up the pile of dirt with the dust pan and broom she had in her pudgy little hands. "It's fine, young man. Just fine." She tossed what she picked up into the trash can under the counter, and huffed back behind the curtain.

"You bet it's fine," Noah whispered to himself.

"I heard that, Mr. Presley."

The bell above the door saved Noah from having to explain his own sassiness to the older woman. *Guess some of Abigail's tartness is rubbing off on me.*

"What are you smiling for, son? It can't possibly have

anything to do with Edna Mae coming back, I'm sure."

Noah pointed at the curtain, and then put his finger up to his mouth to shush him. It did no good. Samuel's robust laughter echoed off the walls and Noah knew he smiled along with him, as well. Seeing his old friend and his much improved mood from the last time he'd seen the unhappy couple made Noah's soul rejoice.

"Old man, you'd do good to keep quiet." Mrs. Collins thrust out of the backroom with her arms laden with jars of beans and vegetables. "Noah if you can pull yourself away from jabbering, I need you to stock those empty shelves over there." She pointed to the far corner of the shop.

"Before you go having him do some work, Edna Mae, I need some coffee."

"Coming right up, Samuel."

At the end of the day, after Edna Mae left, Noah got around to placing the merchandise on the shelves. He couldn't get back to it after Samuel came in. The mercantile came alive with activity and it never died down.

Noah had caught his breath a few times during the day and stood back and marveled at Mrs. Collins and her ability to clean-up the mess he'd made of his place while she was gone. Then how she sold more than he could ever do in one day's time.

"Samuel's right, she could sell dirt to a farmer." He laughed to himself.

"Son, are you talking to yourself?" His father came out of the back of the mercantile. His overall's covered with dust and grime.

"Pop, what are you doing here?" Noah stepped back and his lighthearted mood evaporated.

His father strolled to the middle of the mercantile and gave Noah a backward glance, but didn't answer his question. Instead, the older man proceeded over to the stove and sat down next to it. He took out his pocket knife, looking as if he was ready to clean the mud out of his soiled boots.

"Pop, don't you dare do what you're fixin' to do. There's a place to do that and it ain't here. Mrs. Collins just…" Noah left the rest of the sentence dangling since the look his father gave him said he'd overstepped the boundary.

"First of all, Mr. Think-You-Know-It-All." His pop stood up and came to stand next to Noah. "I can come into this mercantile any time I want. If you don't remember, I'm your father."

Noah hadn't forgotten.

"And another thing," he continued, "I'd say you jumped to conclusions here. I didn't plan on making a mess without cleaning it up." He flipped his pocket knife shut and shoved it into the bib of his overalls. "Son, where are your manners today?"

Honestly, Noah didn't know where his spunk came from, so any answer he gave his old man wouldn't suffice, especially after not seeing him for over a week.

"Well, cat got your tongue?"

"No, Pop. Sorry for yelling at you."

"Thanks. That's better." Noah's father settled back down unto the stool.

Noah stared at the man who he knew as his pop, but it couldn't be him today. Pop wouldn't let his feistiness go so easy. With one word, his father could scalp your hair off before you knew you needed a haircut. Noah exhaled and asked. "So, Pop, did you get your business done in Denver this time around?"

"Son, why don't you come over here and sit a spell." The older Mr. Presley leaned back on the stool. "I need to discuss that very subject with you. Got a minute?"

Twenty-Two

"Gramps aren't the Rocky Mountains the most beautiful thing you've ever laid your eyes on? The Lord sure knew what He was doing the day He created them." Abigail hoped buttering up the scenery would make him forget about taking them away from there.

"Missy, I believe our Heavenly Father has done a masterful work here. Yes, indeed." Gramps led Dancer over to a grove of aspen trees and tied him to one of them. "By the way, dear, you can quit trying to sell me on Colorado. I'm pretty much sold. Now all we have to do is convince your mama."

Abigail jumped off Herkimer and raced over to her grandfather and hugged him. "Oh, Gramps, I knew when you set your eyes on this glorious place it would grab you, too."

"Remember, dear, your mother won't be as easily convinced."

Even in all of Abigail's excitement, she wanted to ask him why they'd have to convince her. What about him buying the opera house? But she decided not to press the issue right at the moment, just revel in the fact she was staying put in her favorite place on earth.

"Gramps, I know what would convince Mama. We need to get her out here. I know she'd change her mind then." Abigail smiled. "When Papa and I came to this spot I think he thought I plain ignored him. Honestly, I didn't, but I couldn't concentrate on a thing he said when we stood on this spot. My eyes, heart and mind were too busy drinking in God's beauty and splendor."

"And you'd sing for your papa, too. I'm certain." He put his arm around her.

"I couldn't help it, Gramps. The words flooded out as if a dam broke upstream. Torrents of living water poured over my soul."

"But you're still keeping your talents hidden under a rock, aren't you?"

"Mama's been talking to you, hasn't she?"

"Ever known your mama to stay quiet for long?"

Abigail chuckled. "No, but I hoped she wouldn't bombard you with the insignificance about my singing just days after you arrived in Central City."

"Granddaughter, never call your special gift from the Lord insignificant. Nothing from Him should ever be classified in that pretense. Through Him, Abigail Jane Thompson, you can do all things."

"Truly, Gramps, I meant no disrespect, but I'm not sure He meant that verse for me." Abigail fiddled with the woolen shawl draped around her neck. Under the deep folds she found the hidden treasure—the precious locket her papa gave her before he died.

She touched the tiny silver locket and felt certain she'd

never take it off, even if she had trouble believing the verse for herself.

Again tears escaped down her cheek, but this time the words encased inside the locket seared deep into her heart. She could almost hear her father saying Philippians 4:13 to her, "I can do all things through Christ which strengtheneth me."

"Gramps?"

"What, my sweet Abigail? Tell your grandfather all about it."

"The day Papa died he gave me this locket." Abigail showed him the gift. "I can open it and the verse is there. "So, why don't I believe the words when it comes to my singing? I believe them in every other area of my life, but Gramps, right now how can I do all things through Christ when my heart is broken into little pieces? I miss Papa so much."

"Which is understandable, granddaughter. I miss him, too." Her grandfather hugged Abigail then said, "And that is why he left you with the verse. It was the lesson he carried with him through his life for all to see. His testimony etched deep within him."

Her grandfather took a step back from Abigail and grasped her hand in his. "Abby, he wanted the same for you because he loved you so much. Whenever I saw you together, I've never known anyone closer than the two of you. From the day you were born, Otto doted on you like some exotic jewel he'd harvested out of the ground. Worth more than gold, silver and diamonds combined. You were dearly loved."

"Oh, he did make me feel special. We had some grand times together, especially out riding. I guess today when I saw you next to Dancer, that sight about finished me off. Papa and I loved taking the horses out here." Abigail paused for a moment and let the crisp mountain air wash over her.

"Gramps, on our rides, we poked fun at Mama. Mostly about me escaping from my music lessons so we could go out and ride. I'm not so sure she always appreciated our shenanigans, but we sure did." Abigail knew her smile reached almost from ear to ear remembering the special memories.

She watched her grandfather as she wove the precious tales of her and her papa. His gray eyes sparkled as tears erupted and ran down his cheeks. Abigail felt certain some came out of the love he'd had for his son-in-law. The rest from the funny stories she acted out with ease.

"Your mama never did have much of a sense of humor, did she? We'll have to work on her."

"Ah huh. She does need help in that area. Especially concerning Noah Presley." The mention of his name made her heart flutter.

"Your mama's been telling me about you and Mr. Presley."

"Gramps, I'm not sure what she's said, but there's nothing going on between me and the store owner. We're simply acquaintances. That's all."

"The look on your pretty little face tells me different. I'll have to go and meet the young man who's captured my granddaughter's heart."

"Oh, Gramps. You don't know what you're talking about." Abigail reached up and grabbed Herkimer's reins and got on him. She took off and didn't stop until she hit the outskirts of Central City. She turned in her side-saddle and watched as her grandfather came riding up next to her.

Once he got up beside her Abigail could see Gramps wanted to ask her something, but it seemed he needed to catch his breath first. A minute went by and he finally said, "I'm not sure what you've been up to, but I'd like to know your secret."

"Gramps, can you keep something under your hat? 'Cause if Mama finds out about it she'll forbid me from riding Herkimer ever again."

"This sounds serious."

Abigail readied herself for a quick take-off. After she disclosed the unthinkable, she might need to leave in a big hurry. "Gramps, are. . .you. . .ready?"

"I'm all ears."

"I'm a better rider because I stole a pair of Papa's pants. I've been coming out here, almost every day, riding just like the gentlemen do."

"You what?"

His expression told Abigail all she needed. She turned Herkimer to the right and galloped towards the livery stable in the center of town. Never once did she glance back to see if her grandfather followed her.

Well, at least this made Gramps forget Noah Presley, but I hope he calms down before he gets back. Don't want him telling Mama. She will surely put us on the next train to Dallas.

"Noah, you remember me talking to you about Matthew Tappen, don't ya?" Noah's father leaned forward on the three-legged stool. A satisfied smile crossed Pop's weathered features.

"No, don't believe you have talked to *me* about him." *Or anyone else, for that matter.*

"Son, I know I have. Anyway, Matthew went with me to Denver. We found out the price of lumber's coming down, so we'll start fixing up the opera house sooner than we thought.

Maybe next week."

Noah jumped up from the stool and went over and poured himself a cup of coffee. Then he didn't drink it. *Think, Noah, think. You've got to tell him everything you know.*

"What has gotten into you, son?"

"Nothing, but Pop, you can't do that. There's someone trying to…"

"Someone's trying to do what, Noah?" His father peered over his spectacles before he leaned back again. "Will you come over here and sit down? You're making me nervous."

Noah had no intention of parking his hind-quarter anywhere near his father. When Pop found out about Matthew Tappen and the banker's late night meeting at the opera house, he preferred to be as far away from his old man as was humanly possible.

"Out with it, son. Now!"

Noah didn't have a choice. The time had come. He'd just say it out loud and get it over with. "Pop, I think someone's trying to swindle you."

This time Noah's father shot up off his own stool and came and stood a few inches from him. They faced each other, toe to toe and almost nose to nose. "Who is it?"

Noah retreated a few steps from his father. Memories of the fear that gripped him at the opera house flashed in his mind. He took a deep breath, and then blurted out the whole story of the clandestine meeting he'd witnessed there the month before.

Cyrus stood still. His eyes not even blinking for what seemed like forever. Noah knew lots of stuff rambled around his pop's head 'cause he looked mad enough to take a person's head off. *Oh, Lord, protect me. I've got more to tell him.*

"Pop, there's something else." Noah strolled over to the

counter to get the ledger.

"Where'd you find this?"

"I didn't find it, Pop, I took it from your room."

His father snatched the book out of Noah's hand. "Thought Edna Mae Collins was Central City's only snoop." The older man sat back down on the wooden stool.

"Can I explain?"

"I suppose." His pop took his glasses off and started polishing the lenses.

"When I caught Mr. Tappen and the banker in the opera house, I tried to tell you, but—"

"But what, Noah. You've had plenty of time to tell me, but instead of talking to me, you stole my ledger."

"Pop, if you'll let me finish my story, it'll make more sense why I took it."

"I sure hope so. Go on."

"Truth is, I tried to talk to you, but either you were heading to Denver with Mr. Tappen. Or when you did come into the mercantile, somebody always kept showing up."

"No excuse to steal my stuff, son."

"No, it isn't, but when I couldn't talk to you, I thought I'd go to the next best source. Your ledger. You keep everything in there. I hoped it might shed some light on who and what Matthew and the banker were talking about that night."

"Did you find what you wanted?"

Deep in his soul Noah hoped the Lord would choose this moment for His triumphant return. Nothing short of His coming back would save him from having to answer his father's question.

"Well, son, I'm waiting. 'Cause what you've said so far doesn't tell me why you took my ledger. If you kept it for a month, there must have been some valuable information in it.

I'd like to find out if you found what you were looking for."

"Not exactly, but there were a few interesting entries in your ledger." Noah decided to move further away from his pop. Be a safe distance apart when he asked—just in case. "Pop, by the way, who is JAR Corp.?" he paused, letting his father chew on his question for a bit.

"A company back East." Pop crossed his arms over his ample chest.

Is that all you're going to tell me? You're going to make me pry it out of you, aren't you?

"And?"

"And, what?"

He watched a slow smile creep across his father's face. The fury gone, the game between them began. Noah decided two could play at this. "Pop, I know you're selling the opera house to JAR Corp. I just haven't figured out why you're still dealing with Matthew Tappen. How much do you know about him anyway?"

The older man's smile faded. "Well, until a little while ago, I thought I knew him and the banker quite well. Didn't know that they would go behind my back. Must have underestimated them."

"What do you think they're doing?"

"I wish I knew, but now that Mr. Reardon is here he and I will get to the bottom of whatever is going on."

"Abigail told me her grandfather wasn't someone to mess with when it came to business dealings."

"Oh so you've been discussing my ledger entries with the little lady?"

"Not exactly, sir." Noah started to pace when he saw his pop's humor left the building.

"If that's not the case, why would Abigail Thompson have

a need to say this about her granddad?"

"Pop, it's kind of funny. Well, not exactly." *Why do I keep saying that?* "When her papa died, she and I had a talk and she said she didn't want to go back to Dallas. She wanted me to help her find something to keep her and her mama here in Colorado."

"So sharing my ledger got this accomplished?"

"That's the 'not exactly' part. She comes over here and announces she's found the perfect plan. She wants to buy the opera house. Her mama would definitely stay then. But, this was where I had to tell her why she couldn't purchase the place. Someone else was buying it."

"JAR Corp., which is her grandfather. So that's why he told me to keep it quiet. Suppose to be a surprise for his daughter."

A laugh almost escaped before Noah caught it. "Anyway, Pop, I didn't know JAR Corp. belonged to her grandpa. So you've got the whole story now."

"Son, there's still one thing I don't understand. Why did you take my ledger?"

Noah knew the truth would come out sooner or later and today would be the day. "The main reason I took your book. . .I wanted to find out what you were doing with the opera house."

"Why's that?"

"I wanted to buy it, Pop. Restore it back to when Gram had it." Noah wished he'd sat down before he blurted it out. Now he wasn't sure his legs would hold him up. "I've been saving to buy it from you."

"Why didn't you tell me you wanted it?"

"Pop, truth be told, you scare the bejeebers out of me."

"Not sure what 'bejeebers' are, but I'm sorry son. You

should have come and talked to me."

"Guess I missed my chance."

"Never know, Noah, sometimes things have a way of working themselves out."

"Doesn't look like it this time." Noah walked over to the wood stove and stoked the fire. "I think I'm going to call it a night. See you in the morning."

"Goodnight, Noah. Glad we finally talked."

Twenty-Three

"Daughter, you're cooking is as delicious as ever." Gramps pushed himself away from the kitchen table and sighed. "If I don't watch myself, I'll have to see if the mercantile carries a belt in a bigger size."

"I'm glad you liked the pot roast." Mama smiled. "I know it's your favorite. Now, would you like some tea? We can take it to the parlor?"

"Sounds good, my dear."

"Say, Gramps, I've got a better idea. Maybe if you help me with the dishes, your supper might settle itself better." Abigail laughed as she reached over and picked up his plate. But her giggling came to a halt when she saw her mama's expression out of the corner of her eye.

Ah oh, Mama wants to talk to him. I bet I'm in trouble.

"Your grandfather doesn't need to help you clean up, dear. You're capable of doing the job without any assistance." Her mother took the dish towel and placed the damp cloth over Abigail's arm. "Here you go."

"Thanks, Mama."

As Abby busied herself with the dinner dishes, she grumbled under her breath. She questioned when she'd have another opportunity to talk to her gramps about a number of things. Namely, the secret she'd revealed on their ride and what Noah told her about the opera house. These two items couldn't be mentioned in front of her mother, or it would send her into a twitter. Heaven forbid, she didn't want that to happen.

"He's going to be *so* mad when he finds out."

"Who's going to be mad?"

Abigail spun around, almost knocking her grandfather off his six-foot frame. "Gramps, you scared me."

"Sorry, but I couldn't help overhearing you. Who were you talking to?"

"Myself."

"Bet it makes for some interesting conversations between the two of you." Her grandfather grinned.

Abigail chuckled and touched his sleeve. "Yes, Gramps, sometimes it does."

"Well, granddaughter, I'm here now if you want someone *else* to talk to."

"What happened to you and Mama having tea? Thought she wanted to chat."

"After we sat down she changed her mind. She scooted me out, saying she wanted to catch up on some sewing project for Christmas."

Abigail felt certain her grandfather made up a story so he could come talk to her. And, however it happened, she needed to find the right words to bring up the subject of the opera house. If they had time, she'd surely revisit the topic of her wearing pants. Try to make it a little clearer.

"How about we slice off a piece of this chocolate cake and sit down." He grabbed two clean saucers and cut off a couple of generous pieces and took a seat at the table.

"Thought you were worried about your waistline, Gramps?"

"Tomorrow. There's always tomorrow."

Abigail hung the dishrag over the sink and sat down next to her grandfather. He didn't wait for her and took a sizeable bite of his cake. But before he completely swallowed it, Gramps started to say something then stopped. Unlike Noah the other day.

"So, dear, who's going to be mad when he finds out?"

Abigail considered her grandfather's question and decided to plunge ahead. "Gramps, about the pant—"

"Dear, if you're worried I'm mad about the trousers you're wearing, I'm not. Seems everything's changing as it gets closer to the 1900's. Why not allow women to wear man's pants?" Gramps laid his fork down and took a drink of his tea.

"I'm surprised you'd say that."

"Out here the fashions are a tad different than in Dallas. Abigail, if it's more comfortable to ride, so be it." He picked up his utensil and jabbed another bite of cake.

Relief washed over Abigail with the one subject spoken of, but the major one still loomed out in front of her. She still didn't know what to say other than to just say it. "Gramps, thanks for not being angry about my clothing choice, but I know you're going to fume and fuss about what I have to tell you about the opera house."

"The opera house? Why is the dilapidated building a concern of mine?"

"Well. . .ah." *Lord, he does know he's buying the thing, doesn't he?*

"Abigail, please enlighten me. I promise I won't fuss and fume.

"Gramps, sit down."

He glanced up from his spot at the table, his eyes narrowed. "I *am* sitting down."

"Oh, you are, aren't you?" Abigail's attempt at laughter came out more like a loud hiccup.

"Granddaughter, the longer you wait to tell me, the madder I might decide to get."

Abigail shared with her grandfather what Noah Presley found in his father's ledger and about the late night meeting inside the building. She left nothing out, even adding the part where she'd asked Noah to help her buy the famed opera house.

Her grandfather stood up and slapped the kitchen table. "Well, I'll be." He broke out in uproarious laughter.

"You better shush or Mama's going to come see if you're having a fit, or something." Abigail got the sentence out and her mother appeared in the doorway. A concerned look on her face.

"Father, what are the two of you doing in here?" Abby's mama eyed both of them with a quizzical look.

Abigail stole a glance in her grandfather's direction, hoping he'd have a better answer than she'd ever come up with.

He winked at her, and then straightened his vest around his ample middle. "Ivy, my dear, your daughter tells the best stories. I never tire of hearing them."

Mama tapped her pointed toed shoe on the wood floor. "Is that so?"

"Uh huh." Gramps hid his smile behind his napkin.

"Then, daughter, you'll have to come into the parlor and

tell me a story or two." Abigail's mother smiled. "Yes, dear, it's been some time since I've laughed so heartily."

A giggle bubbled up inside Abby, but instead of sharing a tale or two with her mother, she decided she better make a quick exit and said as she left, "Sorry Mama, it's time for me to go to bed." She ran past her and her grandfather and didn't stop until she reached her bedroom.

Abigail walked over to her dressing table and sat down. She dabbed at her eyes and started to undo her long blond hair. A soft ringlet fell across her neck. Thoughts of Noah Presley came to her mind. Ever so subtle he'd touched the lone curl, which had escaped from under her bonnet. She couldn't help but smile. The memory made her stomach do somersaults.

Try as she might, she couldn't figure out why the man made her feel the way she did. Now, if they so much as touched fingertips—her heart went all aflutter. Suddenly she couldn't wait until tomorrow. She'd go to the mercantile and tell Noah what happened that evening.

"Wait a minute. Nothing happened. Gramps didn't tell me anything. I don't think Noah will find any of what I tell him very interesting. Especially the part where I forgot to ask Gramps if he's buying the opera house."

Abigail made her way to her bed and tucked herself in under three comfy quilts. The winter winds whistled outside her windows, making her bedroom seem colder than normal. After much deliberation inside her head she got back up and put two more logs on the fire, hoping they would last through the night.

As she started to climb in bed she heard a door shut. *Gramps.* Her curiosity piqued and no matter if cold floors and possible exposure to frost bite met her in the hallway, she'd venture out on a late night trek across the hallway.

Her door creaked when she opened it, but before she lost her nerve she tiptoed the few steps to the extra bedroom. Abigail shivered as she tapped lightly. She almost turned to run back to her room when her grandfather opened his door.

"Well, hello dear. Would you like to join me in my sitting room?" Her grandfather stepped back inside. "I can tell by your expression you have some questions that you'd like me to clear up for you."

Abigail nodded her head as she closed the mahogany door behind her. "You bet I have some questions, Gramps, and the first one is why you laughed at me downstairs." Her sassiness came out a little bolder than planned.

"Your detective work surprised me." Abby's grandfather chuckled again as he walked over and stood facing the fire. "Cyrus and I thought we had a pretty fail safe plan. Guess we underestimated you and his son."

"So, Gramps, would you like to enlighten me on your *plan?*"

He turned to face Abigail. "Can you keep something under your hat?"

"Gramps, you're using my line."

"I know. I liked it so much, I decided to borrow it." He smiled and continued. "Granddaughter, can you keep a secret?"

"Yes, yes, yes. Gramps, you can tell me anything."

"Well, you know most of it. Your Noah—"

"He's not mine." Abigail could feel her cheeks getting red and the roaring fire a few feet from her wasn't the culprit.

"As I was saying, Noah risked his life the night he went to the opera house. But I'm glad he did. Cyrus and I suspected Matthew Tappen and the banker. We just didn't have the evidence to send them up the river."

"Whoa, Gramps. I think you've left out the part about the 'secret.' Or did I miss something. Why don't you start at the beginning?"

Gramps took his watch out of his pocket and flipped it open. "Abigail, I have a better idea. Why don't we stop right here tonight? In the morning we'll go talk with Noah and I won't have to tell it twice."

"You can't possibly be serious, Gramps. I'll never fall asleep not knowing the end of the story. You've got to tell me."

"No, I think it's best we go to bed now. Goodnight Abigail." Her grandfather headed to the door and opened it again.

"You're serious?"

"Uh huh."

Abigail marched out of her grandfather's sitting room, but what she'd rather have done was pester Gramps until the early morning light, if that's how long it took. Instead, she entered her room and flung herself across her bed and pounded her fist in total frustration. "Now what am I supposed to do with myself for eight hours? I know I'm not going to sleep."

She turned over and spied her Bible on the night stand and knew exactly what she'd occupy her time with. She and the Lord had some talking to do.

Twenty-Four

"What did Pop mean when he said 'things have a way of working themselves out?'" Noah couldn't imagine anything concerning the opera house working in his favor.

Noah sat down on the edge of his bed and put his elbows on his knees, his chin resting on his hands. "Lord, You say all things work together for good to them that love God. Well, Lord, I love You, but nothing's worked so far."

A tear trickled down his cheek and he swiped it away with the back of his hand. Noah realized Abigail's grandfather dashed any hope he had of owning the opera house. Along with his own stupidity of not talking to his pop sooner.

"Oh this is nonsense. If I don't get to bed, I won't be worth a hill of beans tomorrow. And with Mrs. Collins I need to be on my toes for anything and everything she throws my way."

Noah quit talking to himself and lay down, but sleep kept its distance. A sure sign he and the Lord weren't done chatting.

He flung his long legs over the side of his bed and got up and grabbed his worn Bible. He opened it to Romans 8:28. The verse he'd quoted earlier. This time he read the whole thing.

"And we know that all things work together for good to them that love God, to them who are the called according to his purpose."

"Lord, what is my purpose?" The minute Noah uttered the question, an image of Presley Mercantile popped into his head. "This can't be what You've called me to do? Me, run a general store for the rest of my life? There must be something more."

Silence filled his bedchamber, but he sensed the Lord telling him *yes, but wait and see how things work themselves out.*

Noah closed his Bible and put it on his side table next to his hurricane lamp. When he turned back to his rumpled bed, it seemed to reach out to him. He slipped in between the covers and before his head hit the down pillow he was fast asleep.

Abigail glanced at herself in the mirror of her armoire the next morning. Blond curls darted in every direction and none in an orderly fashion. Along with her tangled mess on top of her head, the dark circles under her blue eyes announced to everyone she hadn't slept a wink the night before.

"Oh, Mr. Noah Presley is sure to find me attractive today when we go to the mercantile." She turned her attention to tending to herself and wondered why such an absurd statement entered her mind. "Likely, he won't notice me at all. He'll be enamored with what Gramps has to say." Or what she hoped her grandfather would finally tell them about the opera house.

What his intentions for the old rattle trap are?

"And furthermore, I can't believe Gramps wouldn't tell me, but I can't worry about that at the moment. I need to get myself presentable or I won't be there to hear what he has to say." A sharp knock halted Abigail's chatting to herself.

"Granddaughter, are you talking to yourself again?"

She laughed. "No, Gramps. You're hearing things." She rushed over and opened the door and gave her grandfather a hug.

"Good morning, to you too, dear." He smiled as he smoothed down her unruly curls. "Thought you might be angry with me for not telling you. And I do hope you slept well, despite the ominous ending to our meeting last night."

"No. Let's say I have had better night's sleep, but it gave me and the Lord time to talk about some things."

A slight smile turned up the edges of her grandfather's lips. "Sometimes late night is the best time to listen to His still small voice. Now, dear, you better hurry if you're going with me to the mercantile."

"I'll be ready before you can get downstairs and pour yourself a cup of coffee."

Abigail scurried back into her bedroom to finish. Her grandfather wasn't one to wait and the thought of seeing Noah put an extra spring in her weary steps. After a little cajoling with her blond curls, the tangles settled and she dressed in one of her black outfits.

"So, Gramps, are you ready?" Abigail announced as her boots hit the floor of the front foyer.

"Where do you think you're going off to this early in the morning?" Mama's voice rang out from the parlor.

Abigail wished she'd kept quiet until she found her grandfather. But, sometimes words overflowed before logic entered her mind. She couldn't figure out why Mama always showed up when such things happened.

The tension in Mama's voice wound a bit tighter as she added, "Daughter, I'd like your answer before Christmas."

"Ivy, she's accompanying me over to the mercantile." Gramps winked at Abigail. "I believe it's time she introduced me to Mr. Presley, since she's smitten with him."

Abigail wanted to drop into the nearest hole. "Gramps, I beg to differ with you. I am not taken with the young man. He's much too old for me." With each word she spoke in defense, she could feel her cheeks getting redder.

"That's probably a good idea." Mama came and stood next to her father. "Noah does seem taken with our Abigail. I don't know how many times Otto told me how much he liked the young man. I'm still not sure."

Mama's words angered Abigail, but she kept quiet. Her untimely sassiness would get her in more trouble than she wanted this morning. Instead, she rejoiced in knowing her papa liked Noah and she knew her grandfather would too.

"So, Gramps, are you ready?" Abigail touched his arm, hoping her words would spur them towards the front door.

"Yes, dear, I am." Gramps took her hand and placed it within the crook of his elbow. "Let's be on our way. Mr. Presley and I have much to talk about."

Abigail nodded, and then reached up and touched the locket her papa gave her. The Lord blanketed her tired soul once again with His peace. Her unspoken prayer for strength in all things enabled her to walk with her grandfather to the mercantile.

"Well, look who's coming across the street." Edna Mae

Collins peered through the window as she pretended to dust the curtain.

"Who's crazy enough to come out in the morning cold?" Noah laughed when he realized the person making the announcement had done the same thing an hour before.

The bell over the door jingled and the sight of both Abigail Thompson and Mr. Reardon answered his question.

Mrs. Collins brushed her hands on her skirt and extended a hand. "Mr. Reardon, I heard you arrived. I'm so glad to finally meet you. I've heard so much about you. You don't know how sorry I am to hear about your son-in-law. He will be missed, even though the family was only here a short time."

Noah knew the moment the older woman uttered her first words; he needed to get her somewhere other than there. Not close enough to take notes if they discussed what he hoped they would.

Mrs. Collins jabbering climbed all over Noah's nerves, but it gave him ample time to fetch the list he'd made out. He'd send her over to her husband's office to order food stuff. Nothing odd about sending a telegram to get peas and beets on a Wednesday morning.

"Can you two excuse us for a moment?" Noah gently pushed Mrs. Collins back behind the curtain.

"Mr. Presley, do you mind?"

"Yes, I do, but right now I need you to do me a favor." He went on to ask her to take the *important* order over to Samuel and have him send it off to Denver as soon as his fingers could tap it out.

"But you…"

"But, Mrs. Collins, you do it so much better than I." Noah wanted to laugh, but kept quiet. Didn't want to stall the woman's departure.

The older woman grabbed her woolen coat off the hook and stormed out of the back of the mercantile. Before Noah could close the back door, his father pushed it open again.

Great. Now I have Pop to contend with.

Abigail wasn't sure why Noah scooted Mrs. Collins out the back door, but didn't want to complain. If the older woman heard anything she thought newsworthy, the town would know before her and Gramps took a drink from their coffee mug.

And speaking of coffee. "Gramps, would you like a cup of some of the best coffee on this side of the Rocky Mountains?"

"The *best* coffee this side of the Continental Divide," Noah said as he came from behind the flowered curtain. Abigail couldn't help but notice his pop followed close behind him into the mercantile. Both frowning as they entered.

"Son, you didn't tell me we had visitors." Noah's father seemed to perk up as he extended his hand. "Good morning, Mr. Reardon. Miss Thompson."

Abigail only nodded in his direction. She wanted to get down to business. Wasn't that why they'd come to the mercantile in the first place? Now her gramps didn't seem in too big of a hurry to tell the rest of his story and he'd kept her in suspense long enough.

She tapped her fingers on the counter and glanced at Noah. His smile returned and kept her occupied while the older men finished their chattering and handshakes. It also caused her heart to go all aquiver.

"So, what brings you two. . .Well, heavenly days." Noah's father peered out the front window. "It looks like Matthew Tappen is paying us a visit, son, and he doesn't look happy about it."

Twenty-Five

The mention of Matthew Tappen's name caused quite a stir inside the mercantile. Abigail watched as all of them scurried around the store like a bunch of mice being chased by an ornery farm cat. No one going anywhere in particular.

"He doesn't know we're on to him, so let's keep quiet." Gramps whispered as he hurried Abigail's way.

"Son, do me a favor. Tell Matthew I'm meeting with the banker. I'll see him at the opera house at noon."

"Pop?"

"Just do as I say." Mr. Presley hurried toward the back of the store, but stopped. "Jacob, I suggest you and Noah come over, too. Let's see if we can catch this guy red-handed."

Abigail listened and all she could think about was the fact she wanted to kick someone. Mr. Matthew Tappen seemed the likely candidate, with his appearance at such an inopportune time.

Another person on her list—Mr. Cyrus Presley for

ignoring her and leaving her out of the meeting.

All these facts, and not getting to hear the rest of her grandfather's story made Abby hopping mad. And as Mr. Tappen made his way into the mercantile, she noticed they all gaped at the sight of him.

Matthew touched the side of his neck and tilted his head from side to side before he said, "What are all of you staring at? Did I grow another head on my way over here?"

"No, we were just..." Abigail let her words trail off when she noticed his face didn't show any hint of humor.

Noah stepped around the side of the counter. "We were wondering who would be out on such a cold and snowy morning."

"Obviously, me and a few other fools are out weathering the storm." He looked in Abigail's direction. "Oh, I beg your pardon, miss. Didn't mean to call anyone a hoodwink."

"No offense taken." Gramps spoke up while he moved closer to Abigail.

"Good. Didn't mean any harm." Matthew took out his handkerchief and wiped his forehead. Without saying another word, he moved about the mercantile, picking up items then putting them down.

Abigail kept her eyes on the young man. Try as she might, she couldn't imagine such a nice appearing fellow as a crook, but he did seem nervous. She supposed it had to do with everyone gawking at him when he came in. *He's guilty. I just know it.*

The minute the thought came to mind, Abigail reprimanded her quick judgment of the man. After all, what did she know. She'd only heard about Mr. Tappen from Noah. Never having had any dealings with him on her own.

Noah might have made a mistake about him. Let his

overactive imagination play tricks on him that night at the opera house. Maybe the man standing in front of them didn't do anything wrong and they were accusing him without just cause.

"Noah, I'm looking for your father. Have you seen him this morning?"

"Yes. He said he'd meet you at the opera house at noontime."

Matthew glanced at the wall where the clock hung. "Thanks. I'll be going then." But, he didn't move. He just fidgeted, as if he wanted to say something else. He turned toward the door and wiped his forehead again, and then tried to stuff the bandanna into his back pocket. It missed the intended target and fell to the wooden floor. Instead of picking it up, he just kept walking.

"Here, son." Gramps reached down and snatched up the handkerchief. "You might need this. I hear it's going to get kind of warm in the opera house."

Abigail almost burst out laughing at the face Matthew gave her grandfather. The combination between someone who swallowed a handful of hot peppers and a person who got punched in the gut.

Matthew hurried out of the mercantile without another word and the group inside watched his retreat up Main Street.

"Seems something's the matter with Mr. Tappen," Noah commented as he walked over to the shelf housing the pickle jars.

"You might say that. Oh, and by the way I'm Jacob Reardon. Please to meet you, son."

Abigail gasped. "Well, I don't know where my head is. Gramps, I'd like you to meet Mr. Presley."

"Please to meet you, sir, and you can call me Noah. Your

granddaughter does." He smiled and Abigail's heart did a complete flip flop when she spied his lone dimple.

"Since we've made acquaintances. Let's get down to the reason Abigail and I came visiting today." Jacob settled himself on one of the stools next to the counter.

"It's about time." Abigail plopped herself down next to her grandfather and waited, but silence filled the mercantile. "Sorry."

"Anyway, I'd wager Matthew's problem has something to do with your father signing those documents to sell the opera house. Noah, why don't you pour us another cup of the best coffee this side of the Continental Divide and I'll finish the story I started last night."

"And could you hurry up with that coffee." Abby gave him a knowing look. "I've been waiting since midnight to hear the rest of it."

"Abigail, your sassiness isn't going to get it told any faster."

Her grandfather's comment and sideways glance shut her up and she didn't utter another peep. Even when Noah handed her the steaming cup of coffee, she simply nodded. No more unsavory words would pass her lips for the rest of the day. Guaranteed.

"Noah, I did want your father here, but I'm sure he'll fill us in when we get to the opera house."

Which I'm not invited. Lord, this isn't fair.

Abigail sat, with her arms crossed, and listened as her grandfather weaved the tale of the purchase of the opera house. "Otto sent me telegrams, keeping me posted on the happenings here in Central City. When he told me about the opera house and how upset my Ivy got seeing it so dilapidated, we decided to do something about it."

“Papa knew about this.” Abigail forgot her vow to silence. “I can’t believe he never said anything to me.” Tears threatened to fall if she said another word.

“I’m sorry, honey, but we wanted to keep it a secret.” He reached and took Abigail’s hand. “Your papa and I bought the opera house to fix it up for your mother’s Christmas present. He wanted to give it to her, hoping she’d start to love Colorado as much as you and he did.”

Abigail couldn’t contain her tears any longer. They streamed down her cheeks and she smiled knowing she and her mama would now be staying in the place that captured her heart a few months before. *Thank You, Lord.*

“What about Matthew Tappen and Jake Taylor?” Noah paced back and forth behind the counter.

The store owner’s question brought Abigail’s happiness to an abrupt end. Once again she wanted to kick someone. At the moment, Noah topped the list.

“The banker is on our side, Noah. But, when your father told me about the lumberman, I did some checking. Found out he’s wanted from as far west as San Francisco. Officials in New York City are looking for him too. He’s accused of bilking people out of their life savings.”

“Gramps, he sounds dangerous.”

“He is and that’s why we have to be careful.”

Noah stopped pacing and took a drink of coffee. “You say the banker is on the up and up. Sure didn’t sound like it that night at the opera house.”

“Son, speaking of that night. Can’t say that was your brightest day when you snuck in there. Lucky for you—no, luck didn’t have anything to do with it. The Lord protected you after what Abigail said happened to you.”

“Sir. I have to agree. When Matthew opened the door and

it hit my boots and slammed shut. I thought my Maker had called me home."

"I'm glad He didn't take you," Abigail whispered.

"Granddaughter, you shouldn't mumble."

"I didn't, Gramps. Just clearing my throat." Abigail giggled, but felt her cheeks getting warmer with her little fib. She couldn't help but notice Noah. He blushed a vibrant red and his shy smile made her heart beat much faster than it should.

"Can you excuse me?" Noah disappeared behind the curtain.

Noah stood behind the divider and tried to still his heart, which danced around in his chest, threatening to burst forth from where God put it. Any thought of the danger with Matthew Tappen was long forgotten. "Lord, please help me. Miss Abigail Thompson is going to be the death of me."

He kept his voice down as to not draw attention to himself, but he knew if he didn't get back out front, Mr. Reardon or probably Abigail would come get him.

"Mr. Presley, are you alright?"

"Yes, sir," Noah answered the older man.

"Noah, what are you doing back there?"

Before he could answer Abigail's question, he turned and there stood the reason for his escape. Abby held the curtain in her hand and her smile almost lit the darkened storage room. Try as he might, he couldn't say a thing and his breath came in short spurts.

Just when he thought he might regain composure, Mrs. Collins swung the back door open. "Mr. Presley, I might never know the reason you sent me over to Samuel's office, but I sent your telegram. Now, if you don't mind, I have work to do. Pardon me, Miss Thompson."

As Mrs. Collins scooted past them she smiled. Noah decided the smirk on the older woman's face and his closeness to the younger one could spell disaster, so he guided Abigail, by the elbow, back into the mercantile. All the while sparks flew inside his head from touching her arm.

Once he stood behind the counter, Noah's head cleared and he announced, "Mr. Reardon, I don't know about you, but I believe it's time we headed over to the opera house."

"Son, I think you're right. Looks like your store's got all the help it needs. Abigail, you run along. This is men's business and I don't think a lady should be involved."

Abigail seethed at her granddaddy's comment and added him to her list of people to kick when this was all over with.

"And tell your mama that I'll be home in time for afternoon tea."

As Noah followed Abigail's grandfather out of the mercantile, he stole a sideways glance at her. He couldn't help but notice her hands rested on her tiny hips, but her face shone beet red. If he wasn't mistaken, actual fire might be ready to shoot straight out of her ears. He wanted to chuckle since it was the first time he'd known Abigail Jane Thompson to be speechless.

Abigail stood in the center of the mercantile and had no intention of going and telling her mama anything. She intended to follow Noah and Gramps. But before she could make her getaway, she heard Mrs. Collins fiddling with something behind her.

She knew the town gossip waited for the right moment to strike up a conversation with her. And Abby knew if she spent another minute in the same room with the older woman and said anything to her, she'd give her more fodder to tattle about. *Reformed. Oh, I'm sure.*

The minute the last thought hit her consciousness, Abigail repented and knew she needed to say something to Mrs. Collins, but the other woman beat her to it, getting her two cents in before Abby could even open her mouth.

"I'm sure you'll agree with me that Mr. Presley is a fine young man. I'm so surprised someone hasn't snatched him up before now. It must have something to do with him waiting for the perfect girl."

Abigail wanted to interject the impossibilities of that happening, but let the woman rattle on. Figured she'd get a word in edgewise when the time came around the bend.

"Whoever he chooses, she must have good manners."

Laughter tickled Abigail's insides at Mrs. Collins next suggestion. *Guess it won't be me.* Mama would describe her behavior more as high-spirited than having high marks in any kind of etiquette.

"And she must come from a fine, upstanding family."

Abigail straightened her back and smiled. The final description given fit her to a tee.

Mrs. Collins stopped her chattering and stared at her for a moment. "Oh, Miss Abigail, isn't that funny, I just described you. In around about way."

Before the woman could speak another word, Abby jumped in. "Yes, I do think Noah is very nice, but I'm almost certain he's not looking at me for holy matrimony. I tend to be a little too sassy for the likes of him. Have a nice day,

Ma'am." With that said, Abigail turned and bolted out of the mercantile.

Twenty-Six

Try as he might, Noah couldn't figure out why Abigail Thompson seemed so angry when he and Jacob Reardon left the mercantile at 11:15 a.m. On their short walk up Main Street, he rehashed their conversation in his mind, but the entrance to the opera house came before the answer did.

"Jacob. Noah. Over here."

Noah heard his name but couldn't figure out where it came from. He looked around and saw his father peering from around the side of the building, his arms waving as if he was directing a symphony orchestra.

"Pop, what—"

"Would the two of you get over here?" Pops grabbed Noah's arm and the three of them stood behind the opera house.

"Are you going to tell us what's going on or are we going to stand out here and freeze to death?" Jacob tapped his cane on the frozen ground.

"No, but I think we need a plan. Let's go into my office

and talk about it."

Pop led the way across the stage and Noah didn't have any trouble maneuvering it this time. The opera house glowed with kerosene lamps all around. So much easier to see the curtain and boxes stacked almost to the rafters. The two items he'd tripped over in the dark that fateful night.

As they neared the office door, Noah's heart beat a little faster. Now that he saw the area in the light where he hid, he realized how close he'd come to getting caught. For whatever reason, the Lord decided to save him from his harebrained idea to sneak around in the middle of the night.

"Come in here and let's discuss what we're going to do." Noah's father directed them to sit down. "I think when it's close to noon, I ought to go out there by myself and talk to Matthew. Act as if nothing's wrong."

"Cyrus, I have to disagree. He knows something's going on and is nervous. All of us need to confront him."

"He knows me."

Jacob reached into the pocket of his woolen coat and brought out a packet of paper. "I have the evidence of the fabricated businesses he's started up. One of them, alone, will send him away for a very long time."

"Mr. Reardon, that's all well and good, but by the time Matthew is brought up on any of the charges you have in your hand, he'll cut his losses here in Colorado and be gone." Noah's father laughed then added, "Mr. Tappen will be into Wyoming before nightfall."

"Not if the sheriff takes him to Denver."

"Even then, Jacob. You don't know Matthew Tappen."

Noah listened to the men as they bantered back and forth. Neither of their ideas of what to do sounded any better than the other, so he decided to speak his mind for the first time in his life.

"Listen, we all need to settle down. This arguing isn't getting us anywhere. If we jump too soon the three of us could end up getting ourselves hurt. Don't want that to happen to any of us." Noah's louder than normal words silenced the occupants inside of the tiny office.

Jacob Reardon crossed his arms and set the paperwork on the desk in front of him. "Noah you're right. Maybe we do need to rethink this whole thing."

"Son, I don't know what's gotten into you, but I like it."

Noah almost fell out of his chair when his father gave him the compliment. If memory served him right, he believed this might be the first one he'd received in his short life.

"Thanks, Pop."

His father got up and walked over to his desk and sat on the end. "So, Noah, what do you think we should do?"

Noah had waited all of his life for his father to ask him his opinion and the time had finally arrived and he was stumped. *Lord, we're kind of in a hurry. Could You help me here?"*

Abigail continued to fume as she crossed the street. Her muttering escaped out into the crisp mountain air and she cared little if any of the residents of Central City caught her talking to herself.

"This is just grand. Gramps expects me to just run along home like some dutiful child." At that moment her conversation with Mrs. Collins popped into her head. "Well, I told her I wasn't well-behaved and I'm certainly not dutiful. I guess I am spirited. And for that very reason, I'm NOT going home." Abigail glanced around. "Anyway, Mama would ask too many questions I can't answer."

Instead she headed the short distance over to the livery stable. Herkimer stood in his stall and the second he caught sight of her he scampered around. His tail swished back and forth, brushing the sides of the pen. She smiled and stroked his neck and he nudged her with his nose. His dark, charcoal eyes beckoned her and the thought of riding him filled her heart with contentment. The urge to kick someone evaporated into thin air.

"Ready to take her out for a ride?"

Abigail recognized Mr. Price's voice and she turned and gave him a smile. "Yes sir. Today, I'm more than ready."

"How about you get him out and I'll go get your saddle."

Before Abigail could protest he walked over to where they kept them hung. Without a question the gray-haired man reached up and took down Papa's saddle and carried it over and put it on Herkimer.

While he adjusted the straps, Abigail wondered how he knew she wanted Dancer's saddle. Had he seen her out riding and spied the secret she tried to keep hidden under her skirt? Maybe Gramps. . .no he wouldn't say anything concerning what she wore under her riding outfit. She reasoned he'd made a mistake and she'd keep the error under her warm stocking cap.

"Thanks, Mr. Price."

"You enjoy yourself now." He turned and headed back into the livery stable.

Abigail got on Herkimer and the two slowly made their way through town. The fresh mountain air breathed new life into her as she put miles between herself and Central City. She stopped long enough to hoist up her skirt and get down to riding.

Soon most of her ill will about not getting to go to the opera house disappeared, but not all of it. Now, instead of being hopping mad, anxiety gnawed at her insides as she rode along the snow-covered trail.

"Lord, I know this worry isn't from You, but something about this meeting at the opera house isn't right. I'm worried Gramps, Noah and Mr. Presley are in danger."

The minute the last word left her lips, she knew what she had to do. Abigail grabbed Herkimer's reins and turned him to town before he knew what happened. She gave no never mind to her horse or her mode of clothing. All she knew, she needed to get back to Central City as fast as her horse could take her.

"Sheriff Devoe, I need you to come with me." Abigail jumped off Herkimer's back when she saw the man on Main Street. But in her haste she forgot to straighten out her skirt.

"I beg your pardon."

"Please, sir. The Lord told me someone's gonna get hurt. We have to hurry."

The sheriff meandered toward her on the walkway. "Little lady, the Lord don't—"

"Sir, I don't mean any disrespect, but He does and I need you to go in there and grab your gun and come with me." Abigail smoothed her skirt down and headed into the sheriff's office. She waited for the portly gentleman to follow her instructions and if tapping her foot would help him do the job any faster, they'd already be at the opera house.

He didn't seem to notice her impatience. He entered his office and lollygagged while he buckled on his holster, making her want to tell him to hurry it up. Abigail vowed to herself that when she found everyone safe in the dilapidated building, the sheriff would top the list of people she'd kick. But, for right now she had more important things to do and that was to get to the opera house as soon as their legs carried them there.

"Sir, I think we should go in the side door. Slip in quietly. Don't want to alert anyone of our presence," Abigail could tell the moment she uttered the words, the sheriff didn't take kindly to them.

"Miss, if you don't mind, I'm the lawman here. I'll take it from here."

"Fine."

Abigail followed him and she smiled because he took it slow, stopping to look around the back corner of the building before proceeding around it and through the side door of the opera house.

A gasp escaped Abigail when she saw the shambles in front of her. The sheriff spun around and gave her a sharp look and shushed her.

"Do you want to get us killed," the man whispered with a wink.

Lord, this man is doing everything in his power to deserve that kick I so desire to give him.

Part of her wanted to laugh at the thought she just had, but loud voices stopped her merriment and the sheriff and her steps.

"Sir, I told you. Hurry. Someone's in danger." Abigail tugged at his arm to move him forward.

"Miss Thompson, please unhand me."

Abigail complied, but hovered close to the man's side,

trembling from the top of her head to the soles of her feet.

"I suggest you stay right here, miss." He moved away from her. "I'll go investigate and see if anyone's in *danger*."

"It's about time."

The look Abigail received told her she shouldn't have shared her feistiness with him. But him moving toward the loud voices told her he'd deal with the issue behind the door and then get to her later.

As Sheriff Devoe walked across the stage, eerie quiet filled the lighted opera house. The man reached the door and leaned into it as if waiting for more action to happen on the other side. His left hand stood ready on his gun.

"Oh Lord, I did hear Your voice, didn't I?" she whispered.

The minute she asked the question, shouts came from inside the closed room again. Common sense told her to run, but instead her tiny boots carried her across the stage where the sheriff stood.

"I told you to stay put."

Abigail ignored his comment and asked. "What are we going to do?"

"We aren't doing anything. All you're doing is going home." With that the sheriff turned and stormed off in the other direction.

"Where are you going?" Abigail whispered, hoping he heard her.

"None of your concern." The sheriff took off around the corner.

She kept right at his heels and followed the older man as he bound down some stairs and up another set of them. He stopped in front of a closed door and Abigail took a step back away from him when she heard shouts coming from their new location.

The sheriff mouthed the word "stay" and Abigail decided to listen. This time her feet weren't as anxious to go with him. She watched him grab the doorknob and fling the door open.

"Somebody better tell me what's going on before I arrest everyone for just standing in here shouting."

Matthew Tappen spun around. "Back off, sheriff. This don't concern you."

"It does when you have a gun pointed at Noah's head."

"He's not going to shoot anyone."

"Mr. Reardon, shut up or I'll take care of you, too."

"Yeah, like you did Pop."

Matthew backhanded Noah and he fell, hitting his head on the desk on his way down. The sheriff jumped forward.

"That's close enough." Matthew turned the gun on the sheriff.

"Now hold on there, Mr. Tappen."

Tears clouded Abigail's eyes as she watched from the shadow of the doorway she'd snuck up to a moment before. Every part of her being wanted to go help the man she loved and find a way to protect Gramps.

Loved? Where did that come from? Abigail didn't have time to figure it out, but knew she had to do something. And do it fast.

At that moment she remembered the first door they'd stood at. Before she could change her mind, she raced back up the stairs and ran across the stage. As she approached the door, she heard Matthew's loud voice coming from the other side.

"Take one more step and you're a dead man."

Abigail didn't know who Matthew planned to shoot, but right then it didn't matter. All that did were the men in the room. *Lord, You say I can do all things 'cause you strengthen me. Now would be a good time to show me how.* She glanced over at a pile of trash and grabbed the first thing she saw and charged into the room.

"Mr. Tappen you'd do well to put that gun down." Abigail crossed the room, flailing the piece of wood around like she meant to use the darn thing. "Trust me, mister, I'll use this if I need to."

Matthew turned toward Abigail and when he did Sheriff Devoe lunged forward, knocking the gunman off his feet. The two scuffled. Fists hitting their mark on a few occasions.

Without thinking, Abigail raised the board over her head, making ready to take a swing at Mr. Tappen if the opportunity arose.

"Abigail, what do you think you're doing?" Noah scrambled to get up off the floor, but fell back on his behind.

Jacob Reardon raced over and took the plank out of her hand and held it over Matthew and the sheriff. "Okay, that's enough. All of you settle down. *Now*."

Abigail hurried over and tried to help Noah to stand up. Her knees almost buckled when she spied blood trickling down his cheek. She dabbed at his wound with her lace hanky and smiled for the first time since she and the sheriff arrived.

As she held the cloth to Noah's head, she watched the sheriff pry himself away from Matthew's hold. Before Mr. Tappen knew what hit him, the sheriff put handcuffs on him and secured him to one of the chairs.

"You've got it all wrong. They're the ones swindling me. Look at the papers over there." Matthew pointed at the desk.

"Sheriff, he's going to say I signed the contracts with Robert E. Lee's name instead of my own." Noah's father walked into the office. He held his shoulder and Abigail noticed he winced in pain with every step.

"That's exactly what you did. You're a bunch of crooks.

All of you should be locked up for a very long time."

"No, son, it's you who will be locked up for many years. It'll give you plenty of time to think about all the people you've swindled." The sheriff brushed off his shirt and trousers and turned towards Abigail. "And as for you, Miss Thompson, I think maybe you need to spend some time in one of my jail cells for defying my orders to stay put. You could have gotten yourself or any one of us killed."

The reality of what she'd done dawned on Abigail and she gasped. "Oh my, oh my, oh my. Sir, I'm sorry."

"Sheriff, if you hadn't noticed, she didn't get us killed. I do believe she singlehandedly saved our lives." Noah stood up and took Abigail in his arms and held her tight. "And by the way Mr. Reardon, I've been meaning to ask you if I could court your granddaughter. I am head over heels in love with her."

Abigail didn't care if she spent the rest of her born days behind bars. The man she loved just proclaimed his love for her. Nothing else mattered.

Jacob Reardon cleared his throat and Abigail stepped away from Noah. She noticed her grandfather squared his jaw before he began to speak to her.

"Granddaughter, I hate to admit it, but I think your sassiness came in handy today. But will you promise me the next time something like this happens, you'll think long and hard before you act on it?" He smiled and looked over at Noah. "And, son, I give you my blessing because you're going to need all the help that you can get." His laughter filled the room.

"Gramps?" Abigail thought back at the list of people she wanted to kick. Her grandfather moving up to first place with that comment.

"Sorry, my dear."

Matthew Tappen scooted around and tried to stand up, but his attempt to do so failed when the chair caught the back of his knees. He and the seat tumbled to the ground.

"Ouch."

"Sheriff, I almost forgot what we were doing. Why don't you take this scoundrel and put him where he belongs? Looks like Abigail, Noah and I have other business to take care of."

"Mr. Reardon, I'd love to. Cyrus, I need you to go get the banker and the two of you come and give me your statement." The sheriff unlocked Matthew and he stood. The three men walked out of the room.

"Now, how about we go tell your mother our two pieces of good news."

"Gramps, I'm certain Mama will be overjoyed at your news, but I'm not sure she's going to be too happy about my courting Mr. Presley so soon after Papa's death."

"Then I'll go first, granddaughter. I can't wait to see your mother's reaction to her early Christmas present." Abigail's grandfather chuckled as he headed out the door.

Abigail turned toward Noah. "Do you think you're up to sharing our good news with Mama?"

Noah reached down and picked up the discarded board she'd used earlier. "Since this worked so well for you, maybe I'll carry it with me when we tell your mother."

"Won't need it, son." Gramps stuck his head back around the door. "Once I tell my daughter she owns the opera house, and Abigail shares about the two of you, she'll be praising the Lord for all His blessings. Welcome to our family, Noah."

Abigail kissed Gramps then waltzed over and took the board out of Noah's hand and placed it on his father's desk. "There's no need for a weapon. You won over Mama when you brought her an apple pie the first time you came calling."

"I'm not sure about that, but how about we stop by the Teller House and get your mother another apple pie? Just in case." Noah took Abigail's hand in his and squeezed it. "Are we ready to go?"

"Yes, I am." Gramps put on his hat and started for the door.

Abigail ignored her grandfather's comment and snuggled closer to Noah. "Yes, Mr. Presley, we are ready to go, wherever that road may lead us."

"Even if it includes singing at the Central City Opera House when it's restored? Or working alongside me at the mercantile?"

"Wherever it is, Noah, we're sure to make beautiful music together."

About the Author

Janetta Fudge-Messmer is an inspirational author, a speaker and editor. Her first novel, *Early Birds*, came out January 2016, and the sequel, *Southbound Birds* released October 2016. Janetta received Honorable Mention from Writer's Digest Magazine for a fiction article. Her article, "A Working Relationship" was published in Guideposts Magazine. Guide-posts Books published, "Shorthaired Miracle". She resides in Florida, or wherever the wind blows, with her husband of 35 years and their precious pooch Maggie. Janetta, Ray and Maggie became full-time RVers in 2013 and enjoy traveling around the USA in their Minnie Winnie.

Visit her at www.janettafudgemessmer.com, on Facebook (Janetta Fudge Messmer) or Twitter (@nettiefudge).

More From Janetta Fudge-Messmer

Early Birds

Betsy Stevenson is praying fervently for a change. But when a big part of her prayer is answered she asks the Lord, "Is this really You? An RV, of all things."

According to Ben (her hubby and a workaholic), he thinks retiring at 60, buying an RV and traveling is a grand idea. He says, "I've been talking to Matilda (their pooch) and the Lord and I feel it's a go.

After much more prayer and preparation Betsy agrees and they begin the journey to downsize into a 38 foot 5th wheel. Then their RV adventure begins. Their best friends Rose and Larry Wilford tag along and the four get On the Road Again.

Yes, Willie Nelson joins them – if only in song – on the highways and byways of this great country called the U.S.A. While on the road the foursome encounter a near miss with a lamp post, a not-too-happy proprietor at an RV Park, and a 1000 year flood that hits Colorado.

Can the four of them survive their travels together and learn to live, laugh and love more and grump less? Or is the Lord taking them on this path to learn more about themselves than they ever wanted to know? And in the end, do they find it is better to give than receive?

Follow along with the Early Birds on their adventures and I'm sure you'll want to join up with them ASAP. All you need is a sense of humor, willingness to change, And, of course, a recreational vehicle. Any size will do.

Southbound Birds

Rose and Larry Wilford hit the highways on their next RV adventure for more fun, fellowship and fiascos. Ben and Betsy Stevenson follow close behind in their 5th wheel. Jeff and Mary Wells promise to hook up with them when they finish some 'business' in Colorado.

On their way to Ft. Myers, Florida, the foursome make a stop in Biloxi, Mississippi. Soon Rosie wonders if they'll ever put their trucks in gear and get back on the road again. The reason: They've found another church who needs their help.

Rose, Betsy and Mary spend their days as fashion consultants, dressing young women for success (or as Rosie says, "Playing dress up."). Larry, Ben and Jeff, on the other hand, they're up to their eyeballs in sheetrock and mud, and any other handyman task they can find to do.

One thing Rosie's decided, if and when they start traveling toward the Sunshine State, she'll still occupy the passenger seat of the dually. No driving for her. Larry can pester her all he wants.

And the fact her bestest friend, Betsy, drove their albatross on I-10 and lived to tell them all about it, won't change her mind either. The only way Rosie will get behind the wheel is if the Lord, Himself, figures out a way to put her there. 'Cause at the moment, F.E.A.R. is her middle name.

Instead of letting trepidation win, Rose does what she does best…PRAY like a crazy woman. Larry, he's having troubles of his own. His prayer is that their 5th wheel survives his driving and he's not sure it will. One more mishap and he's handing the keys to his wife.

The Early Birds continue to have as many surprises as the road has curves. So why don't you come along, if you dare. Rose, Larry, Ben, Betsy, Jeff and Mary (and some new friends) would love to have you join them in their travels across the U.S.A.

Girly Birds

Keep on the lookout for Book #3 in the Early Birds Christian Comedy series coming June 2017.

The Early Birds pitch in and help proofread Betsy's manuscript, but in the midst of getting it ready for a publisher—a side trip crops up for the women. And it has nothing to do with the Corn Palace in South Dakota. Betsy, Rose and Mary are On the Road Again and their travels include mountains, matchmaking, and mechanical issues. Hope you can hitch a ride with them. Their antics are sure to make you smile.

A Call to Salvation

My prayer while writing *Chords of Love* was for my readers to learn to trust in the Lord. That He loves us and want you as His own—even if you're a tad sassy at times. ☺ If you've finished reading this novella and have never asked Jesus Christ into your heart, I'd like to give you the opportunity to do so today.

> *Lord Jesus, I'm a sinner and I repent of my sins. Please forgive me. I believe Jesus died for my sins and rose again on the third day. Please come into my heart and fill me with Your Holy Spirit. AMEN!*

If you prayed this prayer, you probably have questions about what's next:

1) Find a good church that teaches the Bible.
2) Set aside time each day to focus on God by reading your Bible and praying.
3) Develop relationships with people. Try to find a friend in the church you attend who can help you spiritually.
4) Publicly proclaim your new faith in Christ and your commitment to follow Him by being baptized.
5) Check out this website: www.gotquestions.org. They are there to help you out.

Made in the USA
Middletown, DE
24 January 2021

32311110R00126